This book belongs to:

....

Contents

Illustrated by **John Harrold**
Story colouring by **Gina Hart**
Original stories by **James Henderson**
and **Ian Robinson**
Couplets by **Professor Alan F Murray**
Edited by **Vicky Reed**

The
EXPRESS NEWSPAPERS
Annual

RUPERT

Published by Express Newspapers, The Northern & Shell Building, Number 10 Lower Thames Street, London EC3R 6EN.
A Northern & Shell Media Company. Email: rupert.bear@express.co.uk
Rupert Bear and characters™ © Entertainment Rights Distribution Limited/
Express Newspapers 2006.

No. 71

John Harrold

5

£7.50

RUPERT

When Rupert's father lights a blaze
The room fills with a smoky haze.

It is the start of winter in Nutwood. The evenings grow dark and cold winds blow ... "Time for a fire!" declares Mr Bear. "A blaze in the hearth's just the thing to warm us all up ..." "Oh dear!" says Rupert's mother. "It's rather smoky in here!" "Perhaps the chimney needs cleaning?" declares Mr Bear. "I'll ring the sweep to see when he can come ..." To Rupert's surprise, his father frowns then shakes his head in disbelief. "Next month?" he gasps. "I know you are busy, but we'll have to stop the smoke before then!"

and the Chimney Sweeper

He calls the chimney sweep. "I see ...
You can't come until next month? Dear me!"

Next morning, Rupert finds a smog
Hangs over Nutwood like a fog!

Next morning, as Rupert goes out for a walk he finds someone else complaining about smoke ... "It's very strange!" coughs Mr Anteater. "All the smoke from this bonfire seems to be hanging in the air. It's only old leaves I'm burning, but anyone would think it was wet grass!" Crossing Nutwood Common, Rupert finally escapes from the smoke, which seems to hover over the whole village in a swirling smog. In the distance he spots a familiar figure ... "The chimney sweep!" Rupert blinks. "I wonder if he knows what's wrong?"

"A chimney sweep! I'll ask him why
There's so much smoke left in the sky?"

RUPERT

meets Bodkin

*The sweep looks round. What a surprise –
It's Bodkin ... "Hello!" Rupert cries.*

*"I'm off to test a new machine
Invented to sweep chimneys clean."*

*"There's Nutwood Manor! Soon you'll see
How fast this new machine can be!"*

*"Hello!" says Ottoline. "Come in!
We're ready for you to begin ..."*

As Rupert hurries off after the chimney sweep, he suddenly realises why the man looks so familiar ... "Bodkin!" he cries. "It's you! But what are you doing with a sweep's brush?" "Sweeping chimneys!" laughs the Professor's servant. "At least, that's what we're about to do! This is my master's latest invention. It's an automatic chimney sweeper. We've arranged to try it out at Nutwood Manor. All those old chimneys of theirs should be full of soot ..." "Ottoline's house?" laughs Rupert. "Can I come too?"

As Rupert and Bodkin walk to Nutwood Manor, they talk about the smoky air and how everyone seems to need their chimneys sweeping. "The Professor's new machine will be in big demand." Says Bodkin. "If everything goes well, we'll make a tour of the whole village!" When the pair arrive, Ottoline is keen to see the automatic sweeper. "The Professor has been telling us all about it!" she says. "It sounds marvellous!" smiles Mrs Otter. "Last time we had the chimneys cleaned it took the poor sweep days!"

RUPERT

sees the chimney sweeper

"I think you'll find this fireplace best –
The chimney's perfect for your test!"

"Ideal! The brush spins round, like so,
Then little rockets make it go."

The chimney sweeper starts to rise ...
"It's working!" the Professor cries.

Then Bodkin gives a sudden shout,
"Help! Something's wrong! The rope's run out!"

Ottoline's mother leads the way to a big open fireplace ..."This should be a good test!" she tells the Professor. "It's one of the oldest chimneys in the whole house." "Excellent!" beams the Professor. "Bodkin and I will start work straightaway ..." Rupert watches carefully as the Professor presses a green button. The brush begins to spin, while tiny rockets carry the whole device up the chimney. "Bodkin's rope will stop it flying away!" he calls. "When we've finished, all he has to do is reel it in!"

"Bravo!" cries the Professor as his chimney sweeper disappears inside the enormous chimney. "Unwind the rope slowly, Bodkin. You should feel a slight tug when it gets to the top ..." At first, everything goes smoothly. The spinning brush rises steadily upwards, pulling out extra cord from Bodkin's reel as it goes. "It's making good progress!" he laughs. "We must be nearly finished!" Just then, he feels a tug at his harness and glances down at the reel. "The rope's run out, Professor. What shall I do now?"

The rope pulls Bodkin off the ground.
He leaps up with a sudden bound!

"Don't worry!" the Professor calls.
He pulls Bodkin, then slips and falls.

"The rope broke!" the Professor cries.
"We've left the sweeper free to rise ..."

"The brush!" calls Rupert. "Look up there!
It's flying high into the air."

Before the Professor can do anything, Bodkin is pulled forward, then lifted off his feet ... "Help!" he cries as he disappears up the chimney. "Somebody get me down ..." The Professor dives into the fireplace and grabs his servant's ankle. "Don't worry!" he calls. "I won't let it carry you off ..." As Rupert looks on, he pulls as hard as he can. At first nothing happens – then Bodkin suddenly tumbles down in a shower of soot, landing right on top of his master. "The rope just snapped!" he gasps.

"Are you alright?" asks Mrs Otter. "Yes, thank you," splutters the Professor. "I suppose the rope wasn't strong enough to bear our weight ..." "Just as well!" mutters Bodkin. "I don't mind sweeping chimneys, but I draw the line at going up them with a brush!" "The brush!" gasps Ottoline. "It must still be going round and round!" Rupert and Ottoline hurry out into the garden. "That's the chimney!" calls Rupert. "I can see the brush! It's reached the top of the chimney-pot, but it's still going!"

RUPERT
follows the chimney sweeper

The Professor groans in dismay
As his new sweeper flies away.

The two pals keep the brush in view –
"I wonder where it's flying to?"

As Rupert runs along he sees
The sweeper reach a stand of trees ...

"It's landing!" Rupert gives a call.
"We might just find it after all!"

By the time the Professor and Bodkin emerge from house, the chimney sweeper has flown up into the sky, like a tiny helicopter ... "Good gracious!" cries its inventor. "I'd no idea it could fly!" "It's flying away!" gasps Bodkin. "We'll never see it again ..." "Ottoline and I will follow it!" calls Rupert. "At least we'll be able to see where it goes ..." The pair set off across Nutwood Common, with the chimney sweeper speeding through the sky. "It's got to stop eventually," says Rupert. "The little rockets will run out of fuel ..."

Rupert and Ottoline keep following the chimney sweeper across the common until it reaches the edge of Nutwood Forest. "It's slowing down a bit!" says Ottoline. "We might be able to catch up ..." As the pair reach the forest, they can see the brush more clearly. "It's definitely losing height!" calls Rupert. "I think it's coming down to land ..." The pair decide to keep going in the same direction. "There's a path through the trees!" says Rupert. "We might find the sweeper after all ..."

RUPERT
heads into the woods

The pals search for the lost machine
But find it's nowhere to be seen.

Then Ottoline says she can hear
The sound of buzzing somewhere near!

The pals come to a big old tree
Where Elves stand, staring nervously ...

"Please help us!" cry the startled pair.
"This thing came flying through the air!"

The two pals carry on along the path in search of the flyaway sweeper ... "I can't see it anywhere!" calls Ottoline. "Are you sure we're still going in the right direction?" "I think so!" says Rupert. "It's hard to be certain when you're surrounded by so many trees ..." Just then, the chums hear a strange noise. "Buzzing!" gasps Ottoline. "It sounds like a giant bee!" "You're right!" nods Rupert. "I can hear voices too – they don't sound very happy! Let's go and see what's happening ..."

Rupert and Ottoline make their way through the wood towards the sound of voices ... "Autumn Elves!" gasps Rupert. "They're pointing up to the top of that big tree ..." As the pair step forward they see the Professor's machine, dangling wildly from a length of rope. "The sweeper's still going!" laughs Rupert. "That's what making all the noise. It must have got caught on an overhead branch ..." "Help!" cries one of the Elves. "We're being attacked by a flying saucer!"

RUPERT
follows the Elves

*"Now that the chimney sweeper's found
We need to stop it spinning round ..."*

*"Well done, Rupert!" Calls Ottoline
And switches it off just in time.*

*The Elves ask what the sweeper's for?
"Our Chief needs one of those, for sure!"*

*"Come on!" an Elf calls. "Follow me!
I'll take you down to where he'll be ..."*

Although the chums know that the sweeper is harmless, it is still swinging wildly from the branches of the tree. "How are you going to catch it?" asks one of the elves. "This stick should do the trick!" smiles Rupert. "Stand clear everyone ..." Pinning the sweeper to the tree, he holds it steady while Ottoline reaches for a red button. "Thank goodness!" she sighs as the motor stops. "The Professor's inventions seem to be getting noisier and noisier. No wonder everyone was so alarmed!"

When the Autumn Elves realise that the machine is harmless, they ask Rupert what it is for ... "Cleaning chimneys!" he smiles and explains how it flew away over the rooftops. "I wonder?" murmurs one of the little men. "I think our Chief might be interested in this! Do you mind coming with us? It isn't very far ..." The pals agree and follow the Elf down a flight of steps inside a hollow tree. "How intriguing!" says Ottoline. "I didn't know the Elves had chimneys ..."

RUPERT

meets the Chief Elf

The pals are taken underground
To where the Chief Elf can be found.

"He runs things here, from our HQ
And checks on all the work we do."

Inside the room, alarm bells ring,
"It's smoky – we must do something!"

"A chimney sweeper! Tell me more
It could be what we're looking for!"

At the bottom of the staircase, Rupert and Ottoline see a maze of underground tunnels, each leading off in a different direction ... "Amazing!" blinks Ottoline. "But how does anyone know which path to take?" "It's easy, once you know the way," says the first Elf. "Follow me ..." He leads the pair along a rocky path towards a heavy wooden door. "This is a secret entrance to Elfin Headquarters. It leads straight to our control room. The Chief runs everything we do from there. You'll soon see why we need your sweeper ..."

As they enter the Elves' control room, Rupert and Ottoline are plunged into a sea of flashing lights and buzzing alarms ... "This is dreadful" cries the Chief Elf. "Nothing seems to be working. The smog is still hanging over Nutwood in a great cloud ..." "Visitors, sir!" calls Rupert's guide. "They've got a special chimney sweeping machine that I thought you ought to see ..." "A chimney sweeper!" blinks the Chief. "Now that is interesting. I think this new invention might be just the thing we need ..."

RUPERT
visits the backroom boy

"Our Backroom Boy should really see
Your chimney sweeper – come with me!"

The Backroom Elf is someone who
Invents machines and potions too.

"A chimney sweeper!" cries the Elf
"I wish I'd thought of that myself!"

The Chief asks him to make one too –
"But why? What do your chimneys do?"

The Chief Elf asks Rupert if he can show the Chimney Sweeper to the Elves' Backroom Boy. "He invents all sorts of gadgets for us, but I don't remember anything like this ..." The pals follow him along a winding tunnel that leads to a large, cluttered workshop ... "Come in!" calls a voice as the Chief appears. "I'm just making up a new batch of leaf polish ..." "Sorry to interrupt," says the Chief. "I've got something here that I think you ought to see. It's a marvellous new invention from Nutwood ..."

It looks like a chimney sweeping brush!" says the Backroom Boy. "An automatic sweeper ... I say! What a good idea!" The Chief Elf smiles. "What I want to know is whether you can make one too ..." "Of course!" nods the Elf. "It will need to be bigger, mind you. Give me a few hours and I'll see what I can do ..." "Bigger?" blinks Ottoline. "I thought your chimneys would be smaller than ours ..." The Chief Elf smiles. "Normally, you'd be right, but they aren't ordinary chimneys that need cleaning. These are Nutwood's Smoke Stacks."

RUPERT

sees the Elves' smoke stacks

The Chief says that he'll take the pair
To see how the Elves clean Nutwood's air ...

The two pals look round in surprise
Astonished by the chimneys' size!

"Each chimney gathers smoke and smog.
We turn it into mists and fog."

"A flying brush, like your machine,
Should help us sweep each chimney clean!"

While the Elves' Backroom Boy sets to work, their Chief says he'll take Rupert and Ottoline to see the Smoke Stacks for themselves ... "They look like giant chimneys," he explains. "But they're actually far more important than that. What they should do is keep Nutwood's air clean and fresh ..." At the end of a smoky tunnel, the chums join a big moving staircase which takes them up past a vast complex of pipes and chimneys. "Smoke Stacks!" calls the Chief. "You can see them even better from the top ..."

The pals reach a viewing platform that looks out over the whole of Elfin Headquarters. Smoke Stacks rise high into the sky and each is capped with a huge revolving fan ... "Now you can see how they work!" says the Chief. "Our chimneys don't send out smoke, they gather it in ..." "And they're all sooty!" says Ottoline. "Exactly!" nods the Chief. "We need to clean them so they can turn all Nutwood's smoke into harmless mist. Until then, the whole village will be covered in smog ..."

RUPERT
sees the new machine work

The Backroom Boy soon reappears.
"I've finished the machine!" he cheers.

"Well done!" the Chief Elf calls. "Now we
Can try it out immediately."

The Backroom Boy unwinds the rope.
"This one won't fly away – I hope!"

It's working!" cries the Chief. "You see?
The air is clearing instantly!"

Now Rupert and Ottoline have seen how the Smoke Stacks work, the chief Elf leads them back down the moving staircase to the Backroom Boy's workshop ... To the pair's amazement, he has already finished a copy of the Professor's machine, which he wheels towards them on a low trolley. "Nothing to it, really!" he smiles. "The best ideas are often quite simple. We already had an old-fashioned brush and I was able to use a motor from one of our railcars." "Well done!" says the Chief. "All that's left now is to try it out!"

This will certainly be a test of the new machine!" says the Backroom Boy. "Last time we swept a Smoke Stack it took a whole week. The dirty air leaves so much soot, it's a wonder they don't get clogged more often ..." "Let's go and watch from upstairs!" suggests the Chief. "We'll soon see if the sweeper makes any difference ..." At first, the smog round the chimney seems as bad as ever, but suddenly the fan on top starts to spin more rapidly, clearing the air. "Hurrah!" calls the Chief. "It's working!"

Our chimney sweeper's saved the day!
We'll soon clear Nutwood's smoke away ..."

Please thank the old Professor when
You give back his machine again.

The Chief Elf's special railcar starts –
"Goodbye!" he calls as it departs.

The chums both marvel at the track
Which twists and loops as they speed back.

The Chief Elf is delighted by the success of the new machine. "I can't thank you enough!" he beams. "We'll soon have all the chimneys clear and cleaning Nutwood's smoky air ..." "That's a relief!" smiles Rupert. "I suppose we'd better get back now and tell everyone the news ..." "You should travel back by railcar!" suggests the Chief. "There's plenty of room for the Professor's machine and we can take you right to the edge of the common ..." "Excellent!" nods Rupert. "I expect everyone is waiting for us at Nutwood Manor ..."

"Goodbye!" calls the Chief Elf as the railcar starts off. "Thanks again for all your help ..." Ottoline has never travelled on the Elves' underground railway before and is astonished by the way it twists and turns through enormous, rocky caverns. "It must have taken ages to build!" she blinks. "Yes," says the driver. "Hundreds of years! At first it was a network of footpaths. Then we used ponies and carts and finally railcars ... They certainly make our journeys faster!"

RUPERT
returns to Nutwood

The railcar slows. "We're at our stop!
Just climb this staircase to the top ..."

As soon as they emerge, the pair
Both notice Nutwood's fresh, clean air!

"You're back! Cries Mrs Otter. "We
Had no idea where you could be!"

"My sweeper!" The Professor cries.
"It needs work, but at least it flies!"

The rail journey ends at the start of a steep staircase. "This is one of the main routes to Nutwood Common!" says the driver. "There are 40 different doorways but this is the nearest to Nutwood Manor." Rupert and Ottoline follow him up through the gloom until they find themselves inside a large, hollow tree. "Nutwood!" calls their guide. "You can the the Manor from the top of the hill ..." "Hurrah!" says Ottoline. "We'll soon be home! What lovely fresh air. All that smoke has completely disappeared!"

As they run back to Ottoline's house, the chums see the Professor and Bodkin talking to Mrs Otter. "Thanks goodness!" she cries. "We were about to ask Constable Growler to send out a search party!" "We went searching!" laughs Rupert. "Look what we found!" "Well done!" laughs the Professor. "I'm afraid our first test wasn't very successful ..." "I wouldn't say that!" laughs Ottoline. "Thanks to your sweeper, the whole village has fresh air!"

See if you can make this origami finger puppet of Rupert. You may want to get an adult to help you with the instructions. You can try this with paper that is coloured on one side for even more fun!

3. Next fold both points down so they are touching together at the bottom of the triangle so you end up with a square.

4. Fold up the bottom points to make a set of ears.

2. Then fold in half the other way diagonally.

Tips for folding
- Start white side up
- Begin at step one
- Always look ahead to the next step
- Have fun!

1. Start with a piece of square paper and fold it in half diagonally, then unfold again.

5. Then fold up the single layer of paper over the points and turn the whole puppet over.

7. Fold over the sides and the ears.

8. Next fold up the single layer and turn down the central point at the top.

9. Turn over and draw and colour Rupert's face on the front of the puppet with pens or pencils.

Here is your Rupert finger puppet!

For more information on further origami models please visit the British Origami Society: www.britishorigami.info

This design is © Michael Trew 2006. www.papershake.com

RUPERT

on Um Island

John Harrold

RUPERT
finishes school

"We have a house guest this weekend,"
Says Tigerlily. "Your old friend."

An old and very honoured chum –
The solitary Sage of Um.

No other person shares his home,
And yet, he doesn't live alone.

This riddle puzzles Rupert Bear.
Until a voice says, "Hello there."

School is over for the week and Nutwood's youngsters pour through the gates, chattering happily about their plans for the weekend. "I must hurry home," Tigerlily, the Conjurer's daughter, tells Rupert. "We have a very honoured visitor. It is someone you know – the Sage of Um." "The Sage of Um!" echoes Rupert. "Oh, I must come and say 'Hello' to him." And so the chums set out for Tigerlily's pagoda home.

As they go, Rupert recalls the times he has met the funny old Sage and his flying craft, the Brella. "But, in fact," he winds up, "I know almost nothing about him, not even what Um is." "Oh, I know it is an island and that the Sage is the only person who lives there," Tigerlily says. Rupert wants to ask what she means by 'only person', but by then they have reached her home and he is being ushered in to greet the Sage.

RUPERT

is offered a trip

The Sage is heading home for Um
And asks if Rupert wants to come.

The Sage says, "Come along, my lad.
We'll have to ask your Mum and Dad."

"This Sage seems sensible to me,"
Says Mummy Bear. "So I agree."

Next day the weather's clear and bright.
Just right for an Um Brella flight!

The Sage is delighted to see Rupert. "Why, the little bear who has adventures!" he cries. "Each time we have met there has been adventure afoot." "Not this time!" laughs Rupert. Then Tigerlily chips in: "Honourable Sage, Rupert is very curious about your island of Um ..." At that, the Sage jumps up with a cry of "Then you shall visit it, Rupert! We can go tomorrow and be back for Sunday tea. Let's ask your parents!" So, mind awhirl, Rupert finds himself being hustled to his cottage by the Sage.

Mr and Mrs Bear have never met the Sage and at first don't know what to make of the jolly old man who wants to take Rupert to visit his home. But they have heard Rupert talk of him, he is so charming and Um sounds so nice that they say, yes. And the next morning, with his overnight things in a case, Rupert is hurrying up to the Conjurer's pagoda where the Sage is waiting with Tigerlily and the Brella.

RUPERT

spies a unicorn

So, with a multicoloured trail,
High up into the sky they sail.

They see Um Island, bright and fair,
And Rupert wonders who lives there.

A pony's not a big surprise,
But what's that thing between its eyes?

He gasps to see that it's a horn,
Belonging to a unicorn.

Rupert has travelled before in the Sage's craft, the Brella, and knows what to expect. He has no sooner settled beside the Sage than the Brella is curving in the air, leaving Nutwood a huddle of houses far below. Soon the coast is left behind and they are racing over the ocean. After a while Rupert asks the question he has been longing to ask: "Tigerlily says you are the only person on Um. What else lives on it?" But just then Um comes into sight.

"Oh, it is lovely!" Rupert breathes as the Brella slows and he can really see the island. The Sage smiles and says, "You were asking what, other than myself, lives here. Let's take a look, shall we?" Down goes the Brella in a low swoop. At first there is no sign of movement, then a flash of something catches Rupert's eye. "A pony! You have ponies!" he cries. "No!" laughs the Sage and brings the Brella nearer the galloping creature. Rupert gasps: "It's a unicorn!"

is swept up

"My herd is really quite unique,"
The Sage says. "Come, we'll take a peek."

But then, he feels some kind of trouble
And soars back skywards, at the double.

"My unicorns can't strike a light,
So smoke is not a welcome sight."

Beyond a grove of smoking trees,
Stand unicorns, with knocking knees.

"Yes, a unicorn!" chuckles the Sage. "Now you know what I share Um Island with – a small herd of unicorns, the only ones in the world!" "But where are the others?" Rupert asks. "Indeed, where are they?" echoes the Sage. "The one we saw is the leader and the others usually stay close to it. Let's land near my cave and have a look." So down goes the Brella and it is just about to land when the Sage swerves it back into a climb. "Something's wrong down there!" he says.

The Brella circles back towards the Sage's cave but stops and hovers some way from it. The Sage points to puffs of smoke rising from a nearby clump of trees. "Unicorns can't light fires," he says quietly. "And no one else should be here." Very slowly the Sage edges the Brella closer to the trees. Rupert gasps at what he sees. The trees form a short tunnel leading to a sort of paddock enclosed by rocks. In it, huddled together, are the missing unicorns!

"I don't much like the look of this,"
The Sage says. "Let's see what's amiss."

Then suddenly, it's very clear
What filled the unicorns with fear.

The vile Enchanter's dragon smoulders.
Two large hands engulf their shoulders.

The thug growls, "Come along you two.
My Master wants to talk to you!"

The Sage puts a finger to his lip and points downwards. Rupert nods. They are going to land and must be silent. Gently as a feather, the Sage lands the Brella some way from the trees. The two climb out and head for the puffs of smoke past shrubs and flowers such as Rupert has never seen. When they reach the clump of trees and see what is scaring the unicorns Rupert's eyes pop. It is a fire-breathing dragon. And on its back it has two saddles.

"A-ha!" breathes the Sage. "Now I know who is here! The one who rides a dragon and has long envied me my unicorns …" But at that moment Rupert yelps with fright. He has been grabbed by his jumper. In the same moment a large hand seizes the Sage's collar and a voice booms, "Correct! It is my master, the great Enchanter!" The speaker is a huge man whose head is shaved but for a thin plume of hair held by a ring. He pulls our two towards the Sage's cave.

They see a dark, mysterious chair –
No sign of an Enchanter there.

Until he steps into the light
And Rupert gets an awful fright.

For here's no wizard, old and grim.
A haughty youth sneers down at him.

"Don't mock, you old and foolish man.
For soon you'll learn my master plan."

The huge man bundles Rupert and the Sage into the cave where a lamp casts a pool of light. Around it are deep shadows. Among them Rupert can see a tall chair like a throne. The friends are dumped in the pool of light and the big man addresses the chair. "O, great Enchanter, behold the prisoners you have been expecting." Something rises from the chair. Rupert holds his breath. Then he gasps at the sight of the figure who steps into the light.

"It's a boy!" blurts out Rupert. And, indeed, the 'great' Enchanter, smirking triumphantly, does not look much older than Rupert. But at Rupert's words his smirk vanishes and he screams, "Never, never say that again!" "Say what?" quavers Rupert. "That he is what you said he was," explains the Sage quietly. "He's as old as me. But when he was an apprentice enchanter ..." "ENOUGH!" the Enchanter squeals. "You shall mock me no more, Sage, when you learn what I mean to do!"

RUPERT
is made prisoner

*"I'll weave a growing-older spell.
From horns that you refused to sell."*

*"I'll catch that final unicorn
And then you'll wish you weren't born."*

*"Yon' Enchanter's tale is tragic.
He played with time and messed with magic."*

*"The spell he cast makes boys of men
And now he wants to age again."*

With a nasty grin, the tiny Enchanter reveals his plans: "The most powerful magic in the world can only be made with unicorn horn. I need that magic, but you, Sage, have refused to let me have any ..." "Without horns the unicorns would die!" protests the Sage. The Enchanter sneers: "Well, I need beg no more! When I have caught the one still at large I shall have all the unicorns in the world. Then I shall deal with you. Meantime you'll be locked up."

The Sage and Rupert are bundled into an inner cave where the Sage finishes explaining why the Enchanter never grew up: "He's always been too smart for his own good when he was learning magic. One day, despite being warned not to, he tried out a spell for moving you back and forward in time. He got it wrong and has stayed as he is ever since. The trouble is that he has believed for ages that a potion using unicorn horn will undo the spell he is under."

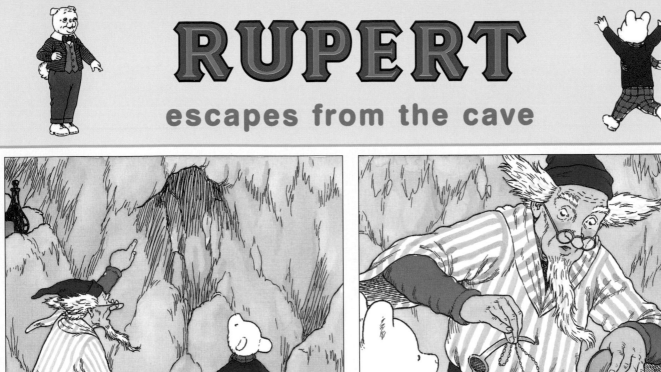

*"That tunnel seems to lead outside.
You'll fit in there. You're not too wide."*

*"Now you must learn to talk, like me,
In unicorn telepathy."*

*"He'll wear this ring. You wear this band.
Then both of you will understand."*

*The Sage and Rupert hatch a plan
To lure the dragon, if they can.*

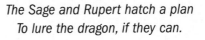

"But enough talk," cries the Sage. "We must save the unicorns. Here's what you must do …" "Me?" squeaks Rupert. In answer the Sage points to a hole in the cave roof. "That lets air into this, my larder. A good small climber could get out that way and find the unicorn leader. Together they might lure away the dragon and free the others. In order to talk to the unicorn …" He produces from his pouch a large ring on a chain and a thing like a headband.

He places the headband on Rupert's forehead and says, "With this on you can 'talk' to the unicorn just by thinking what you want to say. To hear its replies put this ring on its horn and hold the chain." "Maybe I can get the unicorns to attack the dragon," suggests Rupert. "Dear me, no!" the Sage says. "Unicorns are far too timid. You'll have enough to do getting their leader to help you. Now, off you go!" And Rupert starts his climb to the outside.

# RUPERT

makes contact

So Rupert ponders and prepares
To catch the dragon unawares.

A unicorn could lure him out.
Of that, our hero has no doubt.

"I hope the unicorn that's free
Is brave enough to work with me."

He thinks a message through his band.
"Come, unicorn," is his command.

The rocky shaft out of the cave is steep and just wide enough to let Rupert scramble up it. Above him he can see bright daylight and before long he climbs out into the open to find that he is looking down on the captive unicorns. Puffs of smoke from the guardian dragon still rise from the trees in front of them. Rupert can see how right the Sage was about unicorns being timid. They look terrified. "Let's hope their leader's a bit braver," he thinks.

The Sage has suggested that Rupert look for the unicorn leader where they first saw it, and that's where Rupert heads. He thinks, "I'll get the leader to let the dragon see it. If it taunts the beast enough the dragon won't be able to resist chasing it. Then I'll get the others to run for it." When he feels that he has reached the right place Rupert stops and thinks a message to the unicorn's leader: "The Sage has sent me. Come!" There is a whinny behind him.

RUPERT

takes a ride

He slips the ring upon its head
So both can hear what's thought and said.

The beast thinks that it could not dare
To flush the dragon from its lair.

But Rupert 'thinks' a frown, to say
There really is no other way.

It is a risky dragon quest,
But off they go, to do their best.

Rupert and the unicorn stare at each other. Then Rupert slips the ring the Sage gave him over the creature's horn. At once he hears a whimper: "Oh, dear, I'm far too frightened to do it." "Do what?" cries Rupert. "Why, get the dragon to chase me," comes the answer. The unicorn sees Rupert's look of astonishment and goes on, "Remember, while you are wearing the headband I know what you are thinking. And that is what you've been planning to do, isn't it?"

Just as Rupert feared, the unicorn leader is both timid and tiresome. "Why weren't you caught?" he demands. "I'm swifter than the rest and I know every inch of Um," it replies. "Then if you can do it once, do it again," Rupert tells it firmly. "After all, you're the leader. Now, let's go. And to save time I'll ride on your back." He takes the ring and scrambles onto the back of the unicorn. He grasps the creature's mane and off they gallop to the Sage's cave.

RUPERT

starts his plan

With thumping hearts and knocking knees,
They see the smoke above the trees.

"Stay there until you hear my cry,
Then try to catch the dragon's eye.

He sneaks behind the dragon's tree,
Then thinks, "Come, unicorn, to me!"

And as it gallops into view,
The dragon wonders what to do.

Even before the Sage's cave comes into view the timid unicorn is galloping more slowly. When it sees the dragon's smoke above the trees it slows to a trot. And it is very ready to stop at Rupert's command. Using the headband Rupert tells it, "Stay here while I take a look. Listen for my command. When you hear it don't delay. Come to where the dragon can see you and taunt it so it chases you." As he sets off he turns to see the unicorn looking fearfully after him.

Feeling far from brave himself and wishing he were back in Nutwood Rupert steals up on the dragon. Gosh, it is fearsome! With each puff of smoke from its snout the unicorns whinny in fear. "Well, no use wasting time," decides Rupert. He concentrates. "Rupert to unicorn leader," thinks Rupert. Then, with a taunting whinny, the unicorn leader capers into view. Startled, the dragon swings round towards it.

RUPERT
frees all the unicorns

It thunders out to make a chase,
With fury on its fearsome face.

The unicorns are free to go,
But how can Rupert let them know?

As Rupert's thinking what to do,
His headband gets the message through.

The dragon snorts and shakes his head.
Too late, he sees he's been misled.

The dragon can't believe this. A unicorn, one of those wretched creatures, challenging the great Enchanter's dragon! It is so astounded it doesn't move and Rupert wonders if it might refuse to be lured. But just then the unicorn leader gives a particularly offensive whinny. That does it! With one last puff of smoke at the captives, the dragon bounds after its tormentor. "Run!" Rupert shouts at the unicorns.

But they stay put, huddled and scared. Then he sees that perhaps his shouting is confusing the creatures. He presses the headband to his brow and thinks hard: "Unicorns, I am Rupert, a friend of the Sage. I command you to flee while the dragon is away!" Next moment they are racing past him and past the dragon, which has just seen, too late, that it has been tricked. There are so many of them it doesn't know where to turn. The Enchanter and his slave, hearing all the noise, race out of the cave.

RUPERT

rescues the Sage

The young Enchanter and his slave
Come running from the Sage's cave.

The Sage is happy to be free
And smiles at Rupert thankfully.

But then he frowns, as well he might.
The baddies plan a dragon flight.

The unicorns are terrified,
It's time for an Um Brella ride

The Enchanter is squealing with rage as he sees the unicorns disappearing, and Rupert waits until he is well out of the way before he leaves his hiding place and scurries to the cave. One last look after the Enchanter to make sure he has not been seen, then he darts into the cave and makes for the inner chamber. Luckily the key has been left in the door. In a moment the Sage is free and exclaiming, "Well done! Now we must get after that wicked pair!"

Rupert and the Sage emerge from the cave to see that the Enchanter and his slave have mounted the dragon. Rupert almost feels sorry for it, the Enchanter is shouting at it for being tricked by the unicorn. "Oh, you shall pay for this!" he shrieks. "Now, get after them!" He digs his heels hard into the dragon's sides; the beast flaps its wings and takes off. "Quick! To the Brella!" cries the Sage. "We must stop the Enchanter attacking the unicorns at all costs!"

RUPERT
halts the dragon

And, as the dragon clears the trees,
The Brella lifts up on the breeze.

But Rupert looks down in dismay.
The unicorns are easy prey.

He sees the dragon, far beneath –
A thing of fire and claws and teeth.

John Harrold

The Sage and Rupert must give chase
And head straight for the dragon's face.

Rupert and the Sage race to where they left the Brella and scramble aboard. The Sage twiddles part of the Brella's handle and before Rupert can blink the craft is high above the trees. Higher still is the Enchanter's dragon. It moves fast and the Brella is hard pressed to catch up. Before it can, the dragon dives and Rupert sees why. It is heading for the fleeing unicorns. The stupid things have stayed together making themselves an easy target. If only they had scattered the Enchanter wouldn't have known which way to go.

Now he has them. "Attack!" he screams. "Stop them anyhow!" Breathing flames, the dragon swoops on the terrified unicorns. "Hold tight!" the Sage cries and the Brella dives, faster and steeper than the dragon. Just when it seems the dragon's flames will scorch the unicorns, the Brella swoops under its snout and the great beast, with a startled roar and flappings of wings, has to swerve aside.

RUPERT

and the Sage fall

The beast pulls back, the chums await.
Will it run, or retaliate?

In seconds, they are in no doubt.
The dragon simply tips them out.

And, as they have no parachute,
The Brella has to substitute.

They land quite safely, and unharmed.
But soon have cause to be alarmed.

The unicorns have been saved from the dragon's attack, and Rupert can see them scatter among the trees. For a moment, too, it looks as if the Enchanter is giving up the chase, for his dragon seems to be heading away from the scene. In fact, he's far from done. The dragon is only giving itself room to attack. It makes a great sweeping turn then heads for the Brella. Before the Sage can get it out of the way the Brella is swiped by the dragon's great wing and is capsized.

Then everything happens at once. The Brella turns upside-down. The Sage grabs the handle. Rupert catches the Sage's hem with one hand and with the other his case which has been in the Brella all the time. Down they float with the Brella as a parachute and Rupert trying very hard not to show how frightened he is and how much he wishes he were safe at home. But they reach the ground unharmed. Unfortunately, at the same moment so does the dragon!

RUPERT

is in danger

The young Enchanter's full of rage.
"I've caught you now, you useless Sage!"

But then they see the unicorns.
With angry eyes and deadly horns.

Confusion fills the dragon's face.
He finds himself pinned into place.

The chief of unicorns looks grim.
And now the dragon's scared of him!

The Enchanter smirks. "You have often crossed my path, Sage," he pipes. "And until now have always won. Now I am going to get rid of you and this bear. Then I will recapture all the unicorns and the magic of their horns shall be mine." Rupert daren't think what is in store for him and the Sage. There is a nasty glint in the dragon's eyes. "I'm not going to let them see how scared I am," he thinks. Just then from the trees emerge the unicorns!

Everyone is too astounded to speak. The only sound is the pad of hooves. The unicorns are nothing like the frightened things Rupert last saw. Horns levelled like spears, they close on the dragon. Last comes their leader looking, if anything, more threatening. It halts only when its horn is an inch from the dragon's face. The Enchanter is the first to find his voice. "Don't stand there!" he screeches at the dragon. "I order you – destroy the unicorn!"

RUPERT
is amazed at the unicorn

The young Enchanter calls, "Now – burn!"
The unicorn stands, cool and stern.

Then Rupert gets a huge surprise,
As tears roll from the dragon's eyes.

And, while our heroes are elated,
The young Enchanter's quite deflated!

"You are a beastly little boy,
And this, a nasty little ploy!"

Rupert can't remember having seen anyone quite as angry as the Enchanter. His face is twisted with rage as he squeals at the dragon. "Fire, I say! Destroy it!" Smoke trickles from the dragon's nostrils. The gentle unicorn and the beastly dragon glare into each other's faces. Rupert has to cover his eyes. He waits for the fiery roar. But nothing. He risks opening an eye. And he can scarcely believe it. A large tear is running down the dragon's snout.

That tear is just the first of many, and as the dragon sobs, smiles spread on the faces of Rupert and the Sage. Suddenly all the fizz goes out of the Enchanter and he seems like nothing more dangerous than a particularly nasty, small boy. Now the Sage takes over. "You unpleasant little thing," he storms. "This is our last battle and you have lost, thanks to the gentle unicorns you despised." The Enchanter slumps in his saddle. There is nothing he can say.

RUPERT
understands how he helped

The young Enchanter's quite forlorn –
Defeated by a unicorn.

And as our heroes win the day,
The baddies simply slink away.

"Now," Rupert says, "I want to hear.
How did you overcome your fear?"

"They knew that I was frightened too,
And knew what they would have to do."

"Let them go," the Sage tells Rupert. "This so-called 'great' Enchanter and his dragon have been beaten by the gentlest creatures, unicorns. From now on among magicians and sages his name will just be a joke. I don't think he will stray far from his domain." So, using his headband, Rupert orders the unicorns to fall back. "Begone!" the Sage commands the Enchanter who gulps an order to his sobbing dragon. It lumbers into the air and has soon dwindled into the distance.

The very next thing Rupert does is slip the ring over the unicorn leader's horn and asks, "Well, how did you all suddenly turn bold?" His smile grows as he listens to the reply. Then he turns to the Sage and says. "When I wore the headband they heard all my thoughts, not just those that were meant for them. They know I was as scared as they were but kept going and tried not to show it. So they felt ashamed and decided that if I could do it, so could they. And it worked!"

RUPERT

and the Sage fly home

Soon, though their victory is sweet.
They're gasping for a bite to eat.

"That young Enchanter may, one day,
Grow older in the normal way"

The unicorns stand on the shore
As Rupert flies for home once more,

Where Mummy greets him, on the green,
And asks him what he's done and seen.

With the Enchanter banished and the unicorns free to roam Um Island again, Rupert realises how hungry he is. The Sage is peckish too, and so the pair fly back to the cave for a meal. As they eat, Rupert asks, "Will the Enchanter ever grow up?" The Sage replies, "He could. And it wouldn't need magic. All that's needed is for him to stop thinking and acting like a particularly unpleasant little boy." "And will he?" Rupert asks. "I hope so, says the Sage.

Next day Rupert and the Sage leave for Nutwood. As the Brella heads out to sea, the unicorns gather to see them off. "You taught them something important," the Sage tells Rupert. "You showed them that being brave isn't the same thing as not being afraid." Rupert is still pondering that remark as the Brella sweeps in to land near his cottage. "Brave? Me?" he thinks. "Really?" But what he says is, "Oh, look! There's Mummy and Daddy waiting for us!"

THE END

40

Here are two pictures, which at first glance look identical. However, there are actually 10 differences between the two. Can you find them all? *Answers can be found on page 109.*

Spot the Difference

RUPERT

Spring will come to Nutwood soon.
It's time to weed and sweep and prune.

Mr Bear has decided it's time to tidy up the garden ready for spring. This year, he tells Rupert, he's going to try something special when it comes to trimming the hedge. "Will it really look like a peacock?" asks Rupert. "I hope so," smiles his father. "Let's see what we can do ..." Climbing up to reach the top of the hedge he clips away with the shears until a large, green bird begins to take shape. "This is fun!" laughs Rupert, as he rakes up the cuttings.

and the Peacock Hedge

But Rupert wonders, as he's raking,
Exactly what his Dad is making!

He finds out what the snipping means –
A privet peacock struts and preens.

After a lot of careful clipping, Mr Bear finally announces that the Peacock Hedge is finished. "It's marvellous!" cries Rupert, and hurries inside to fetch Mrs Bear. "My goodness!" she says, when she sees what the pair have done. I thought you were busy, but I had no idea you were up to something like this! It looks so lifelike. If I didn't know better, I'd say it was about to fly away." "I hope not!" smiles Mr Bear. "After all that work I want to enjoy looking at it!"

"He looks quite real." says Mrs Bear,
"Will he fly, or just sit there?"

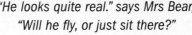

RUPERT

visits Tigerlily

And next day, Tigerlily hears
Of Mr Bear's artistic shears.

"I'll trim this lion hedge as well,
With Daddy's magic pruning spell"

The hedge grows huge before their eyes.
The chums reel back, with frightened cries.

"I'll shrink it back!" says Tigerlily.
"It's just my joke – now don't be silly."

The next day, Rupert visits Tigerlily's house together with Bill, Podgy and Ottoline. He tells them all about the Peacock Hedge and how his father spent all day trimming it into shape. "In our garden we have hedges like dragons and lions," says Tigerlily. "My father keeps them tidy with his magic wand.' "How?" asks Rupert. "Come and see," says Tigerlily, leading the way outside, to a fine green lion. "Watch carefully," she says, then points at it with her wand ...

At first nothing happens, then the lion begins to grow bigger and bigger ... "Gosh!" gasps Rupert as it towers over the startled chums. "Now for a spot of pruning!" laughs Tigerlily and waves the wand again. All at once, the hedge stops growing and begins to shrink back to its normal size ... "Amazing!" blinks Podgy. "It's certainly easier than using shears!" chuckles Tigerlily. "Now let's all go to Rupert's garden. I want to see this peacock for myself ..."

So, much relieved, back home they run,
To where the bird stands in the sun.

Will Tigerlily's incantation
Waken Mr Bear's creation?

The peacock neither moves nor flies
And, with relief, poor Rupert sighs.

But as he celebrates their luck,
He hears a rustle, then a cluck!

When the chums arrive at Rupert's house, they all hurry into the garden to see the hedge. "You were right!" cries Bill. "It's even better than I'd imagined ..." "Perfect!" says Podgy. "I saw a peacock at the zoo last summer ..." "It's certainly very fine," agrees Tigerlily thoughtfully. "But I wonder if it could look even more lifelike?" Raising her wand, she points it at the peacock and starts to chant another spell. "Oh, no!" groans Rupert. "What now?"

To Rupert's relief, the peacock seems unaltered by Tigerlily's spell. "It can't have worked," says Ottoline. "Last time the hedge started growing straightaway ..." "I wasn't trying to make it grow," says Tigerlily. "I wanted ..." she breaks off as the pals hear a sudden rustle of leaves. "It moved!" cries Rupert as the peacock peers down at the astonished chums. "I don't believe it!" gasps Ottoline as the bird gives a loud cluck, and starts to preen its wing ...

RUPERT

watches the peacock fly

Before their unbelieving eyes,
The peacock flaps its wings and flies.

Then, straining every leafy feather
It leaves the garden altogether.

And, leaving Rupert in the lurch,
It finds a tree on which to perch.

He tries to catch it, but in vain.
It flaps its leaves and flies again.

"Now your hedge looks even more lifelike!" laughs Tigerlily as the peacock turns its head to look at the chums. She is so pleased with her joke that she doesn't notice the bird has lowered its tail and started to flap its wings. All of a sudden, it gives a loud squawk and takes off. "It's flying away!" cries Rupert. "That's not meant to happen!" gasps Tigerlily as the peacock clears the garden hedge and disappears from sight. "Come on!" calls Rupert. Let's follow it ..."

Running out of the garden, Rupert soon spots the peacock, perched on a high branch of a nearby tree. "Try calling to it," suggests Ottoline, but the bird shows no sign of wanting to come down. "There's only one thing for it!" declares Rupert and starts to climb the tree. At first the peacock seems curious but as Rupert gets closer, the bird gives a cry of alarm and flies off before he can reach it. "Oh, no!" he groans.

Then Mr Bear's fine hedge creation
Causes Nutwood consternation!

Mr Anteater is shocked, poor chap,
And Nutwood folk are in a flap.

Past Nutwood's shops it makes its flight
And gives poor Mrs Pug a fright.

At last, it lands upon a ledge
Above the grocer's fruit and veg.

By the time Rupert has clambered down, the peacock has flown off towards the middle of Nutwood. How everyone stares to see the strange green bird flapping its way along the High Street! Mrs Sheep gives a cry of alarm as it swishes over her head, while Mr Anteater drops his cane and reels back in astonishment. "That peacock's feathers look just like leaves!" "They do a bit!" says Rupert. "Can't stop, I'm afraid, I've got to keep up to see where it lands ..."

Hurrying down the High Street, Rupert catches up with the others just as the peacock passes the fishmonger's shop. "Good gracious!" gasps Mrs Pug, "I don't believe it!" "Nor do I!" blinks the shopkeeper. Eventually the flyaway bird lands on a blind outside Mr Chimp's shop. As the pals draw near, they see PC Growler approaching. "What's all this?" demands the policeman. "It looks as if that bird's escaped from Nutchester Zoo!"

RUPERT

asks PC Growler for help

"This is," says Growler, "past belief!
A peacock made of privet leaf!"

He tries to catch it, but in vain;
It lifts its leaves and flies again.

"It won't come back unless it's led.
We'll lay a trail with crumbs of bread."

And, fortunately, Mrs Bear
Has many bits of bread to spare.

"Wait a minute!" says Growler. "There's something very odd about this bird ..." "It's a rare breed," explains Rupert hurriedly. "I can see that," replies the policeman. "But what's it doing here in the middle of the High Street?" "It ... it escaped," says Ottoline. "We tried to catch it, but it flew away ..." "Leave this to me," says Growler and reaches up towards the bird. As he does so, it flaps its wings and takes to the air. "Bother!" cries Growler as the bird flies out of sight.

He thinks hard for a moment, then gives a sudden cry. "Breadcrumbs are what you need! My wife's always putting them out for the birds in our garden. If peacocks eat them too, then it's the perfect way to lure him back ..." Rupert is delighted with his suggestion and hurries home to see if Mrs Bear has any stale bread to spare. "Of course," she smiles. "I was saving some in case you wanted to feed the ducks."

So Rupert and his Nutwood chums
Create a trail of tasty crumbs.

The bird decides it's time to eat
Before the trail is quite complete.

The peacock stops to peck and scratch,
As Bill prepares to make a catch.

Bill grabs the bird with all his might,
He pins it down and holds it tight.

Running back to join the others, Rupert sets about laying a trail of breadcrumbs to entice the flyaway peacock. "That's the idea!" says Growler. "Just wait till it sees those ..." "Let's lead it somewhere quieter," suggests Ottoline. "Good idea," agrees Rupert and continues the trail up on to the common. He has hardly finished scattering the last handful of crumbs when there is a loud cry and the peacock comes swooping down towards the chums.

As soon as the peacock lands, it starts pecking eagerly at the breadcrumbs. "What now?" asks Ottoline. "It won't be long before they're all gone ..." "I'll try and catch it off guard," declares Bill. Keeping well out of sight, he creeps round behind the bird, then inches slowly towards it. The moment he's close enough, he leaps forward and grabs the startled peacock before it can fly away. "Hurrah!" he cries triumphantly. "It won't escape so easily this time ..."

This doesn't work for very long.
The privet peacock's very strong.

And, as the peacock makes its flight,
A squealing badger clings on tight.

"Come Rupert!" Tigerlily cries,
"We'll have to follow where it flies."

"If this adventure's to end well
I'll have to try another spell."

As Bill holds on to the struggling peacock, his cry of triumph turns to one of alarm. "It's trying to break free!" he calls to the others. "Don't let go!" cries Rupert and hurries forward to help his friend. The bird starts to flap its wings frantically and squawks crossly, as if it's determined to get away. The next moment, it hops into the air and takes off, with an astonished Bill still hanging on as tightly as he can. "Stop!" calls Rupert when he sees what's happening, but it's too late ...

The chums are all shocked by what has happened. "Come back!" gasps Ottoline as she watches Bill being carried off over the treetops. "We've got to rescue him!" declares Rupert. "Who knows where the peacock will fly to next?" "What can we do?" says Tigerlily. She thinks for a moment, then tells the others she's had an idea. "Follow me!" she calls, running back towards the Pagoda. "It was my magic that started all this, perhaps I can use it to help Bill ..."

This magic bowl out on the lawn
Will make a cloud to fly upon.

"A travel cloud will do the trick.
I'll need your help – come on, be quick!"

"Ten drops of red, ten drops of green
And then we'll see what's to be seen."

Then, right before their very eyes
A fluffy cloud begins to rise.

When they reach the Pagoda, Tigerlily explains that her father has gone out for the morning, so she'll have to try another spell all by herself ... She leads the way to a large metal bowl which stands glinting in the sunshine. "You and I must follow Bill," she tells Rupert. "A travel cloud will carry us across the skies ..." "What's a travel cloud?" asks Podgy. "You'll see!" declares Tigerlily. "In fact, I need your help to make the spell work ..."

The bowl is covered by a heavy grille, which Rupert and Tigerlily stand on while she tells Podgy what to do ... Opening a little drawer, he takes out two bottles full of brightly coloured liquid. "They have to be mixed together," says Tigerlily. "If you put ten drops from one bottle into the bowl, then Ottoline can measure out ten from the other." Soon a thick mist starts to rise. "Good!" smiles Tigerlily. "The spell's working."

It flies above the Nutwood trees
And floats off on a gentle breeze.

'Til Tigerlily turns its head
To where the leafy peacock fled

It flies from Nutwood, green and fair,
Towards the mountains, bleak and bare.

Then, in a glow of glorious light,
The Bird King's castle comes in sight.

As Podgy and Ottoline look on in astonishment, the mist grows thicker, till it forms a cloud which carries Rupert and Tigerlily up into the sky. "Tell my father what's happened the moment he returns," she calls. "We'll be back as soon as we can ..." Peering into the distance, Rupert spots the peacock, flying off with Bill. "After them!" commands Tigerlily and points at the bird with her wand. The cloud spins round, then starts to gather speed ..."

On and on the peacock flies, until all signs of Nutwood have been left far behind. "I wonder where it's going?" thinks Rupert. Suddenly, the bird starts to climb higher, up towards a thick bank of cloud. "We mustn't lose sight of it!" cries Tigerlily and orders the travel cloud forward. As they soar up after the peacock, the pair see the turrets of an imposing castle, surrounded by hundreds of birds. "Of course!" gasps Rupert. "It's heading for the Bird King's palace ..."

RUPERT
arrives at the palace

The other birds all jump with fear.
This is the strangest peacock here!

The chums look worried – as you would,
And hope the Bird King's mood is good.

At least Bill Badger's smile is bright.
He's had a most exciting flight.

The guards can only stare and frown –
The peacock's hopping up and down.

The peacock swoops down and lands in the courtyard of the great palace. All the birds are astonished to see Bill perched on its back, and fly off in alarm the moment the mysterious newcomer arrives. "We'll land in the courtyard too!" declares Tigerlily and orders the travel cloud to stop. I hope the Bird King won't be too angry when he sees us," says Rupert. "He doesn't like strangers visiting his palace and hates the idea of anyone flying except birds!"

As soon as the travel cloud lands, Rupert and Tigerlily hurry over to Bill, to make sure he's all right. "Yes, thanks!" he smiles. "The peacock's quite friendly, really. It landed gently to make sure I didn't fall off." "Why has it come here?" asks Rupert. "I don't know," replies Bill, "But it seems to be having some sort of row ..." As the pals turn round, they see the peacock arguing with one of the King's courtiers. "Oh, no!" cries Tigerlily. "He's summoning the guards!"

The Chamberlain explains, the cause
Is written in the Bird King's laws.

A peacock is not made of leaves.
Such birds are fake, the King believes.

"It's in this book of law, you know.
He can't stay here. He'll have to go."

The King walks by, in splendid breeches.
"Please let me stay!" the peacock screeches.

"What's the matter?" Rupert asks a nearby bird. "The Chamberlain claims that the newcomer's an impostor!" it declares. "He's sent for the Royal Archivist to prove it cannot be a peacock, as it claims." At that moment, a courtly looking bird appears carrying a large book. "Now we'll see!" announces the Chamberlain. "All types of bird are recorded in the King's guide. I'm sure there's nothing about green peacocks who have leaves instead of feathers ..."

"As I thought!" declares the Chamberlain. "This leafy creature can't be a proper bird!" As he speaks, the King arrives and demands to know what's causing all the commotion. The peacock hurries forward and tells him how he's flown all the way from Nutwood to seek admission to the palace. "Please let me stay," it begs. The King looks thoughtful, and then turns to Rupert and Tigerlily. "You are from Nutwood too," he says. "Tell me more about this strange bird ..."

RUPERT

comforts the peacock

Although the Bird King's not unkind,
He can't be made to change his mind.

The poor peacock has been rejected
And looks most mournful and dejected.

"Come back to where you were created.
That's where you'll be appreciated."

And Rupert's words are not in vain.
The peacock struts with pride again.

The King listens gravely as Rupert tells how the peacock came to life, escaped from his garden, and finally flew off with Bill on its back. "I thought as much!" he says. "I'm afraid the Chamberlain is right. Although this strange creature looks like a bird, it cannot stay here, after all." When the peacock hears the King's words, it makes a low clucking sound and hangs its head sadly. "Poor thing!" says Tigerlily. "It seems such a shame."

Rupert kneels down to talk to the sad peacock. "Never mind," he says gently. "You can always come back to your old home in Nutwood. We all think you're very handsome. And besides, you'll be the only peacock in the whole village!" The peacock looks up, then starts to preen its leafy wings. "Will you come with us?" asks Tigerlily. "Yes," the peacock nods. "Bravo!" declares the King, and summons two of his swiftest eagles to lead the visitors.

RUPERT
returns to Nutwood

They head for home, without delay.
And eagle escorts lead the way.

When Nutwood Common comes in sight
The leafy peacock leads the flight.

The Conjurer says that he can tell
The peacock's under someone's spell.

"You must not use your wand for fun.
One day, you might just hurt someone."

When everyone is ready, Tigerlily orders the travel cloud to rise, with Rupert and Bill perched safely aboard. "What a splendid way of flying!" cries the King. "Much better than those noisy machines you normally use." The peacock gives a squawk of farewell, and then flies off with the King's eagles guiding the way. Before long, Rupert spots Nutwood below. "Let's see if my father has returned yet," says Tigerlily, steering the cloud down towards the pagoda."

The moment the peacock lands, an angry Conjurer strides into the garden. "So this is the strange bird all Nutwood's been talking about!" he declares. "Another of my daughter's mischievous spells, I presume ..." "I'm sorry," says Tigerlily. "I didn't mean any harm ..." "Magic should never be taken lightly!" says the Conjurer. "Luckily, all is well, but in future you must take more care." As he turns towards the peacock, his frown gives way to a broad smile.

Then chums and peacock have a race
To find the peacock's proper place.

"Now, peacock, perch upon that ledge.
I'll turn you back into a hedge."

A wand is waved. A spell is cast
Then bird and hedge are one, at last.

"That bird looks real, I can't deny.
It really looks like it could fly!"

"I must admit, it's a clever spell!" says the Conjurer. "No wonder everyone was so surprised." He thinks for a moment, then tells Rupert to lead the way back to his garden. As the peacock runs along behind Rupert and Bill, it seems delighted to be returning home. "That's right!" smiles the Conjurer as it flutters up on to the hedge. "I want you to sit perfectly still, while I try and make a spell." Pointing his wand at the bird, he slowly starts to chant a rhyme ...

For an instant the air is filled with shimmering stars, then the peacock returns to being part of the hedge. The next moment, Mrs Bear appears and greets the visitors. "Hello," smiles the Conjurer. "Rupert was just telling me all about your new hedge and I had to come and see it for myself!" "It is rather good, isn't it?" says Mrs Bear. Very lifelike!" says the Conjurer, winking at Rupert. "Very lifelike indeed ..."

THE END

Rupert's Wordsearch

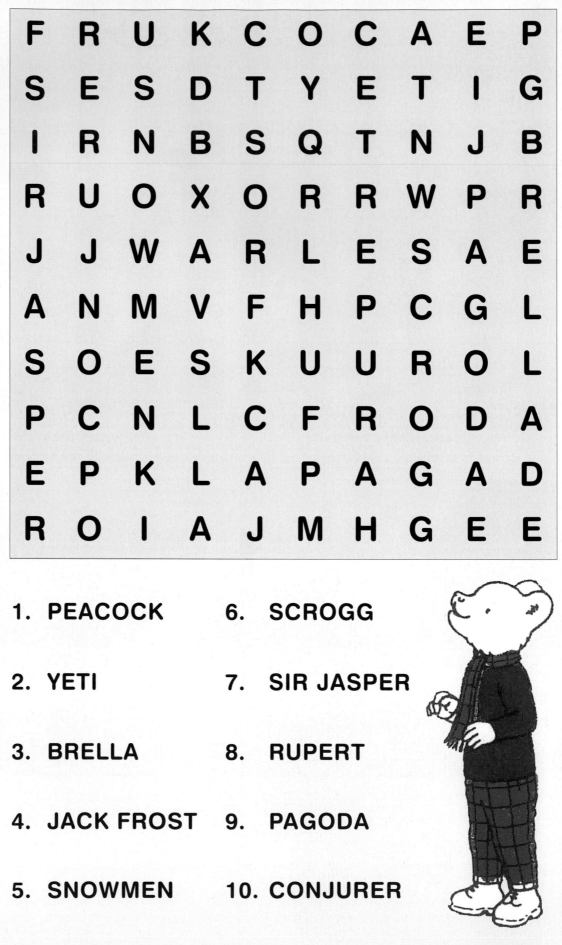

F	R	U	K	C	O	C	A	E	P
S	E	S	D	T	Y	E	T	I	G
I	R	N	B	S	Q	T	N	J	B
R	U	O	X	O	R	R	W	P	R
J	J	W	A	R	L	E	S	A	E
A	N	M	V	F	H	P	C	G	L
S	O	E	S	K	U	U	R	O	L
P	C	N	L	C	F	R	O	D	A
E	P	K	L	A	P	A	G	A	D
R	O	I	A	J	M	H	G	E	E

1. PEACOCK   6. SCROGG

2. YETI   7. SIR JASPER

3. BRELLA   8. RUPERT

4. JACK FROST   9. PAGODA

5. SNOWMEN   10. CONJURER

Hidden in this puzzle are 10 words and names that you will find in the stories. See if you can find them all. The words can be across or down and even backwards! *Answers on page 109*

RUPERT
and the
Present Mix-Up

HAPPY CHRISTMAS RUPERT. SORRY ABOUT THE MIX-UP.

John Harrold.

RUPERT

and Bill head home

Says Rupert, "I can't wait to see
What Santa Claus will leave for me."

"I've asked him for a model boat."
"How odd." laughs Bill. "That's what I wrote!"

"A pile of parcels – just for me.
They're stacked beneath the Christmas tree."

One parcel's round, one parcel's square,
But Rupert's speedboat isn't there.

Rupert and Bill are so excited about Christmas. They have both been playing with their friends out in the fresh, wintry weather. As they head homeward on Christmas Eve across Nutwood Common they are both talking about what presents they are hoping for and also how much they would both love a model speed boat for Christmas. "We will have to meet with the others on Christmas Day," says Rupert. "Then we can all see what presents Santa has given us!"

On Christmas morning Rupert is awake early, investigating his stocking presents. They're lovely, of course, and he does appreciate them and he will enjoy them. But what he is so looking forward to are the presents under the Christmas tree. Oh, it must be there, the model speedboat he has his heart set on! But when he rushes downstairs he sees none of the packages under the tree are the right shape and size to be the oh-so-wanted speedboat!

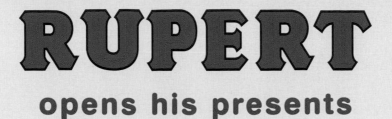

So, trying not to feel too miffed,
He finds a small and heavy gift.

This speedboat motor will not float –
Bill Badger must have got the boat.

His chums have also got strange things –
A railway tender and some wings!

Podgy wonders, with a sigh,
If toys might be in short supply.

Rupert tries not to look disappointed about the speedboat. There's sure to be something just as good. He picks up a parcel which is small but quite heavy. "What is that?" asks Mrs Bear when it is unwrapped. "A-a motor for a speedboat," Rupert gulps. "What! And no boat to put it in?" exclaims Mr Bear. After a moment Rupert says, "I know what must have happened. Bill Badger and I both wanted speedboats. I suppose Santa only had one and split it between Bill and me."

Rupert has arranged to meet his pals at his garden shed after breakfast to show off their main presents. Algy and Podgy are there when he turns up with the speedboat motor. Willie, Bingo and Bill haven't arrived. Glumly, Podgy and Algy display their presents, the tender of a model engine and the wings of a model aircraft. Rupert knows that Algy and Willie both wanted an aircraft while Bingo and Podgy wanted engines. "I suppose, like the speedboats Bill and I wanted, Santa had only one of each," he sighs.

For all the presents are the same –
Half a toy or half a game.

They all agree, in gloomy mood,
That Santa did the best he could.

So Rupert smiles and helps his Mum,
To keep them both from feeling glum.

He hides the motor in his coat,
To give to Bill, to power his boat.

When the rest of Rupert's pals arrive they also look a little glum. They are carrying the parts missing from Rupert's, Podgy's and Algy's presents. Rupert is sure that Santa must have run out of presents and has shared them between his friends which he explains to the others. They all try to disguise their disappointment and agree that Santa did this for the best. Then after arranging to meet the next day they take their part-presents home.

At home Rupert says nothing about what his chums got for Christmas and for fear that talk of others' presents may upset him, Mr and Mrs Bear don't ask. They don't think he's right about Santa dividing one present between two but they can't think what has happened. Now they have another puzzle – Rupert himself. He was thoughtful when he came in but now he perks up as if he has made a decision, and after tea he says he is going round to Bill's house. When he leaves he has something tucked under his coat.

gives Bill the present

Soon, Rupert runs back home, to find
That his chum Bill is just as kind.

For Bill has faked a Santa-note
And given Rupert his new boat!

Next morning, all the Nutwood boys
Meet up, with different halves of toys.

The bits of speedboat, plane and train
Have all been swapped around in vain!

In no time at all Rupert is back from his trip to Bill's. He is about to let himself in when his foot scrapes against something on the doorstep. It's a parcel and even in the poor light of a winter teatime he can tell from the shape what is in it. He calls to Mrs Bear to tell her he's back and smuggles the parcel upstairs to unwrap it. Of course the label is meant to make him think it has come from Santa. But he knows better. "Oh, dear, Bill," he sighs. "It seems that great minds do indeed think alike!"

Next morning, remembering that he and his pals have arranged to meet again, Rupert takes the speedboat hull from his toy-cupboard and goes out to greet them. As he emerges from his garden gate they come running up and like himself, each is clutching the part that was missing from his main present. They make a big show of being excited about what they've got now. But, still, no one has a complete main present. And it doesn't take them long to guess why. Six pairs of lips start to twitch.

RUPERT
laughs at the mix-up

They look perplexed but, shortly after,
Fall about with roars of laughter.

"Let's meet tomorrow," they agree,
"To share our presents properly!"

And, as the chums from Nutwood play,
They hear a jingling, airborne sleigh.

"Hello there, Rupert, Podgy, Willie,"
Santa says, "I do feel silly!"

Of course, they all see what's happened. Each has given up the bit of the present they received to help his chum make a complete present. They all dissolve into laughter. "How we didn't bang into each other, all rushing about exchanging presents, I just don't know," Rupert gasps. When they have caught their breath again the six agree that they will work out some way to share the presents. As they break up to take their part-presents home Rupert calls after them, "Let's all meet later and go sledging on the common!"

Having taken their part-presents home, Rupert and his pals head for the snowy slopes of the common with their sledges. Despite – or perhaps because of – the presents mix-up with each trying to help each other, they are in high spirits. Suddenly a whoosh, a tinkle of bells and Santa's sledge has joined theirs! He climbs out. "Lucky to find you together – all those who got only part of their presents," he booms. Rupert and the others goggle at him, open-mouthed, as he strides up with his present sack.

*"New elves came to work for me
And botched the packing thoroughly!"*

*He laughs to hear how, overnight,
The chums had tried to put things right.*

*"Ho, ho!" laughs Santa. "Never mind.
It comes from trying to be kind."*

*"Happy Christmas and well done.
Most muddles aren't quite this much fun!"*

Rupert and the others, still astounded at suddenly finding Santa with them on Nutwood Common, can only gawp as he undoes his sack. "I'm terribly sorry about the mistake," he tells them. "I've had new people working in the packing department and, what with the rush of work, they got into a muddle. But I've brought the parts you need for your presents." With that he starts to hand out the part that each gave to his friend! And he smiles when Rupert points this out to him.

"No, not another mix-up!" Santa beams at the puzzled pals. "I know you well, and when I found what had happened I knew you'd each try to help his chum, and I thought, what's the point in having all that swapping round yet again? So I've given each what he's lacking now. Right? Then I must be off!" And with no more ado he mounts his sledge and soars away. "What a happy mix-up this has been. Merry Christmas!" laughs Rupert as they wave goodbye.

THE END

Rupert's Coconut Cakes

4oz–100g Butter (at room temperature)
3oz–75g Sugar
1 Egg (beaten)
5oz–150g Self Raising Flour
$^{1}/_{2}$ oz–15g Desiccated Coconut

2 teaspoons of Lemon Juice
Coconut to coat the cakes,
approx 3oz–75g
Glace Cherries cut in $^{1}/_{2}$
(with the help of an adult)

1. Wash your hands before you begin preparing the food and make sure you have an adult to help you.

2. Have a non-stick baking tray ready and have the oven pre-heated to 375°f/gas mark 5.

3. In a mixing bowl, add the butter, sugar and the $^{1}/_{2}$oz of desiccated coconut and cream together with a wooden spoon until they are mixed well.

4. Break the egg into a cup and whisk with a fork and add to the bowl. Then add the flour to the mix pouring in the 2 teaspoons of lemon juice and continue to mix until all ingredients are mixed together.

5. Put the rest of the desiccated coconut into a large dish, and with your hands, roll the mixture into small balls. Then pat them carefully to flatten, and push lightly into the desiccated coconut you have put in the dish. Turn it over and repeat, so both sides are coated with the coconut.

6. Place the halved glace cherries in the centre of each cake. Then put the cakes onto a non-stick baking sheet, then still with the help of the adult that is helping you, place the baking tray in the oven. Make sure they are wearing oven-proof gloves.

7. Bake for 15–20 mins.
Remove from oven and leave to cool thoroughly before eating.

Remember, do not attempt to cook this recipe without adult supervision.

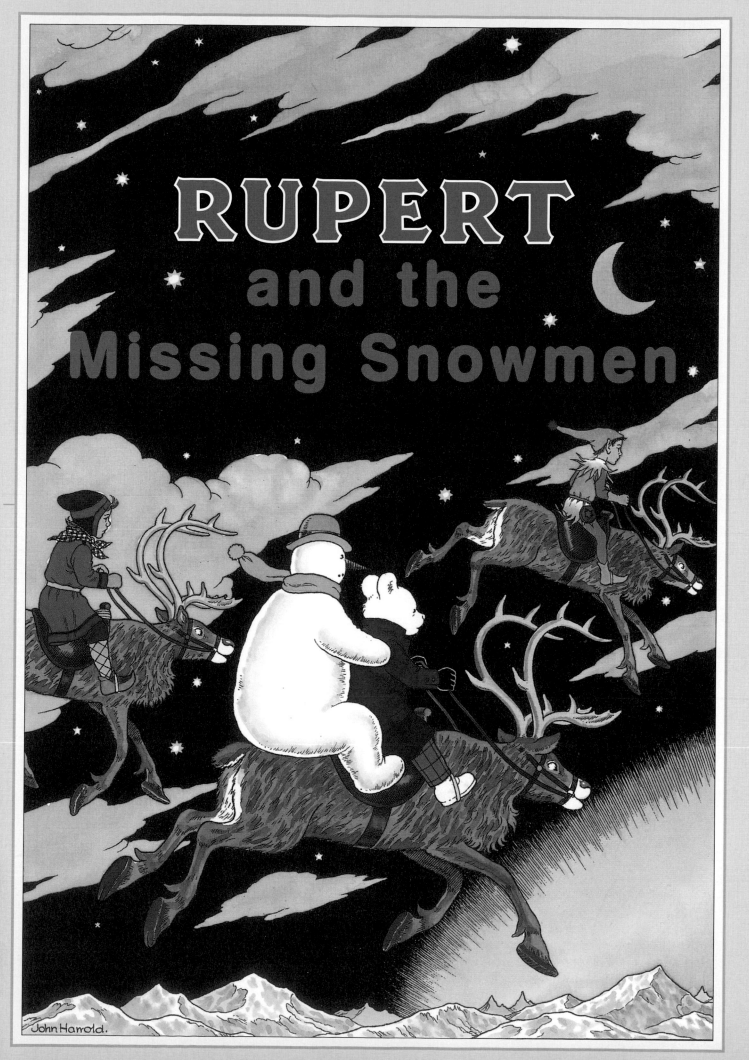

RUPERT
and the
Missing Snowmen

RUPERT
has a friend to stay

*A visitor from Lapland's here.
It's Rika, tending Santa's deer*

*Her reindeer need a place to rest
And Pong-Ping's garden is the best.*

*The friends head for their cosy beds,
With dreams of winter in their heads.*

*But in the night, a howling gale
Brings swirling snow and sleet and hail.*

When Santa's reindeer aren't pulling his sleigh at Christmas, they live in Lapland, where they are looked after by a little girl called Rika. Rupert and Rika are good friends and have agreed that she will stop off on her journey home to spend a day or two in Nutwood. Rupert's parents are delighted to see her when she arrives late one evening, having left her reindeer tied up in Pong-Ping's garden, where there's plenty of room.

Later that evening, when Rupert and Rika take a last look out of the window before going to their rooms, the night is clear and moonlight glistens on the snow. "Doesn't it look lovely," smiles Rupert. "Yes," agrees Rika, "so calm and still." Long after the pair have said goodnight and gone to bed, Rupert is woken by the howling of the wind. Instead of calm moonlight outside, he sees thick snow flashing past his bedroom window ...

RUPERT
sees Billy Blizzard

And, during one ferocious blast,
Rupert's snowman hurtles past!

A well-known rascal's weaving spells ...
In Rupert's head, there's warning bells.

Whatever Billy Blizzard's doing,
Rupert knows there's mischief brewing.

"That's Jack Frost's cousin," Rupert cries.
"Trouble follows where he flies."

Rupert jumps out of bed and opens the window. It is almost snatched from his grasp by the swirling white storm which rages outside. He peers out and gives a cry of amazement as he sees his snowman, which has been standing in the garden, caught up by the storm and carried away on the wind. As the snowman spins past his window, the storm seems to clear and Rupert sees a familiar-looking figure outside, directing the snow with a jagged icicle.

"It's Billy Blizzard!" Rupert's cry rings out above the noise of the wind, and the sinister figure turns to give him a wicked grin. The next minute he leaps up after the tail of the snowstorm and is carried away into the night. "Rupert! Whatever's the matter? Do shut that window!" says Mrs Bear, who has heard Rupert call out. Rika has heard him too and comes to see what's happening. "It was Billy Blizzard!" Rupert cries. "I saw him out there, standing in the garden."

RUPERT

and Rika explore

"He's so bad, King Frost banished him
Off to the South Pole, bleak and grim."

Says Mummy Bear, "That may be true.
But bed's the safest place for you."

Next day, they head off to explore.
And think of Billy's pranks no more.

But then, by chance, upon a hill,
There's Jack Frost, standing very still.

"Who's Billy Blizzard?" asks Rika. Rupert explains that he's Jack Frost's cousin, who was banished to the Frozen South by Jack's father, King Frost, because he kept making terrifying blizzards. "Ever since then, he's been a sworn enemy of the King. That was one of his blizzards just now. It was so strong that it carried off my snowman!" "Well, there's nothing we can do about it now," says Mrs Bear. "Back to bed, everybody. Try to get a good night's sleep."

Next morning Rupert and Rika agree not to spoil the first day of her visit by worrying about Billy Blizzard. As soon as they have finished breakfast, they set off to have a proper look round Nutwood. No one is about as they head across the common to the top of a hill from where, Rupert tells Rika, you can see the whole of the village. They are almost there when Rupert spots somebody scanning the horizon with a telescope. "Look!" he cries. "It's Jack Frost."

RUPERT
meets Jack Frost

Jack greets them both, but he looks grim.
It's clear that something's shaken him.

"I've searched through Nutwood, far and near.
There's not a single snowman here."

Then Rupert suddenly exclaims,
"It's Billy Blizzard's fun and games!"

"Oh no!" cries Jack. "If they are lost,
They can't fly back to serve King Frost."

Jack is so intent on studying Nutwood through his telescope that he doesn't notice Rika and Rupert until they reach the top of the hill. "Why, Rupert!" he exclaims. "I was just about to try and find you. But who's this?" Rupert introduces Rika, who says she's delighted to meet Jack Frost at last. "What did you want me for?" Rupert asks. "I hoped you'd be able to tell me what's happened to all the snowmen around here?" says Jack. "There's not a single one to be seen!"

"I can tell you what happened to my snowman!" Rupert cries. As he hears about last night's blizzard, Jack Frost looks more and more grim. "It's plain that Billy has taken them all to get back at my father," he declares. Rika looks bewildered, so Rupert explains that each year, just before the thaw, Jack comes to collect all the snowmen and take them to his father's palace. "Now I've got to find a way to get this year's snowmen back from Billy Blizzard!" says Jack.

RUPERT

plans a rescue adventure

*"They'll be in Billy's dungeon now.
I'll have to set them free somehow."*

*"We'll rescue them on Santa's deer."
Says Rika. "They're just resting here!"*

*Rupert wants to join the pair.
But first, he checks with Mrs Bear.*

*"The South Pole?" Mummy cries. "Alright.
But do make sure you're wrapped up tight!"*

Jack explains that he's sure Billy Blizzard has taken the missing snowmen to his ice fortress in the Frozen South. "The trouble is, I can't call up a wind to fly there as it's the wrong part of the world." "I'm sure Santa wouldn't mind you borrowing his reindeer," Rika suggests. "You mean you'd really lend them to me?" cries Jack. "Of course, I'd have to come too," says Rika, "to make sure they're all right." "Then so must I," declares Rupert, stoutly.

Although he's keen to join the others, Rupert knows that he has to ask his mother first. "I'll come with you," says Jack as Rika hurries off to Pong-Ping's house to get the reindeer ready. Mrs Bear has met Jack Frost before and knows that Rupert has always returned safely from their adventures together. When she hears what's happened, and that Rika will be going too, she agrees to let Rupert go and help Jack but tells him to wrap up well.

RUPERT
rushes to see Pong-Ping

They run to Pong-Ping's house, to see
Three reindeer, snorting eagerly.

The chums get ready, full of hope,
As Rika checks her herdsman's rope.

They mount their deer as twilight falls.
"Goodbye and good luck!" Pong-Ping calls.

Then off they fly, into the night.
To stars and sunset, clear and bright.

Rupert and Jack hurry to Pong-Ping's house where Rika has prepared three of her reindeer for the long flight to Frozen South. Her face lights up when she hears that Rupert can come too. Pong-Ping has agreed to look after the other reindeer and is introducing himself to Jack Frost when Rupert notices that Rika is tying a coil of rope to her saddle. "What's that?" he asks her. "A reindeer herdsman's lasso," Rika replies. "I always carry it with me on a long journey."

Daylight is fading by the time Rupert and the others are ready to set off. The reindeer usually fly only at night because Santa prefers them not to be seen. But since Pong-Ping's house is well away from the village and as it's nearly dark already, Rika agrees that this time they may start straight away. "Good luck!" cries Pong-Ping as the three chums mount up. "Up and away!" calls Rika and in no time at all the three reindeer are soaring up into the darkening sky.

RUPERT

spots a strange light

And only Jack knows how and where
To fly to Billy Blizzard's lair.

Then Rika calls, "A shooting star!
It's heading straight for where we are!"

And as they wait and wonder why,
It weaves and wobbles in the sky.

But Rupert gasps, and mutters, "Um!
I can't imagine why he'd come!"

Night falls and soon Rupert has the feeling he is flying among the stars. Although Rika is in charge of the reindeer it is Jack Frost who decides upon their course. "How can you be so sure you're right?" Rupert asks him. "When my father banished Billy Blizzard he exiled him to the Frozen South," says Jack. "I know where …" Before he can finish Rika breaks in with a cry of, "Look! There's a strange light ahead of us. What can it be? It seems to be coming this way!"

"Perhaps it's a shooting star?" suggests Jack. "Then it's like none I've ever seen," answers Rika as the light weaves its way towards them. "Too slow and wobbly." To Rupert's surprise the light seems oddly familiar and as it gets closer a thought grows in his mind. "It couldn't be, surely," he whispers. "What did you say?" asks Rika. But Rupert is too excited to answer. For now he is sure he knows what the strange light is. "How extraordinary!" he gasps. "It is him!"

RUPERT
meets the Sage of Um

But then he laughs, "Well, it is true.
The Sage of Um – it's really you!"

"But that poor snowman in your brolly
Looks quite confused – and none too jolly."

"He just dropped in," the Sage replies.
"From stormy clouds and snowy skies."

"I have to head back home to Um,
This Nutwood snowman cannot come."

"The Sage of Um!" cries Rupert. His friends see that the light is really a lantern hanging from the handle of a large, upside-down umbrella in which sits an old man dressed in a long gown. "An unexpected pleasure!" smiles the Sage as Rupert introduces him to Rika and Jack, explaining that the Sage is an old friend. "It's been a night of strange meetings," laughs the Sage and gestures to the snowman who's alongside him. "You'll never guess how I met him!"

It turns out that the Sage was flying towards his home on the island of Um when a blizzard suddenly appeared from nowhere. "I dived down to get out of the way," he explains, "but scraped the underneath of the storm cloud. That's when this snowman appeared. He must have fallen out of the cloud. What am I to do with him?" "Take me back to Nutwood," pipes up the snowman. "I'm afraid I can't," says the Sage. "I have to get back to Um Island without delay."

RUPERT

is joined by the snowman

"My unicorns are ill, you see,
And won't recover without me."

So one of Santa's deer must bear
A snowman and a little bear!

And as the Sage hits the ignition,
The friends resume their rescue mission.

But fear is clear on Snowman's face,
To think of Billy Blizzard's place.

"What's the matter?" asks Rupert. "It's the unicorns!" replies the Sage, who looks after the only unicorn herd in the world. "They've all caught bad colds, I'm afraid. I've got to get back and make sure they're all right." "In which case we'll take the snowman," says Jack. "He ought to be with me, anyway." "He can ride on my reindeer," says Rupert and flies closer to the Brella. The snowman smiles and eagerly clambers up behind Rupert.

"Nice to meet you!" calls the Sage as he whisks away. We must hurry," says Jack. "Forward!" cries Rika and off bound the reindeer. "No! Wait!" squeaks the snowman "There must be a mistake! This is the way Billy Blizzard went!" "Of course!" says Rupert. "We're going after him to make him give back the snowmen he stole from Nutwood ..." "But I've just got away from him," whimpers the snowman. "He might catch me again. Oh, no don't go on, please!"

"You are a coward!" says Jack Frost.
"You don't care that your friends are lost."

At last the dawn brings shafts of light,
That shine upon a chilling sight.

It's Castle Blizzard's eerie glow,
With icy moat and constant snow.

"Let's find a safer place to hide,
To plan how we can sneak inside."

"How selfish!" thinks Rupert. "I'm glad he isn't mine." "Please turn back, Jack Frost!" begs the snowman. "I don't want to be one of Billy Blizzard's slaves." "Nor do the other snowmen he stole!" snaps Jack. "Can't you get him to turn back?" the snowman appeals to Rupert and Rika. But neither replies for, in the growing light, they can see something ahead. "Can that be it?" Rika begins. "Yes," Jack says quietly. "It's Billy Blizzard's fortress."

The reindeer slow to a halt. The whimpering of the snowman is the only sound to be heard as Rupert and the others gaze at the grim ice fortress, which is surrounded by a moat bristling with spears of ice. The only entrance is over a drawbridge, which is firmly closed. There is no chance of flying in on the reindeer, for a constant blizzard swirls fiercely above the walls. "We must land somewhere out of sight and decide what to do," says Jack. The snowman gives a low moan.

RUPERT

and pals hide

They land, but Snowman quakes a lot
Inside the boots he hasn't got!

So Rupert, Jack and Rika hide
Where they can spy, but not be spied.

"These castle walls are made of snow.
They might as well be steel, you know."

"We can't get in, there is no doubt.
So, let's get Billy Blizzard out!"

"We'd be out of sight down there," says Rupert, pointing to a flat stretch of snow behind some ice slabs which face Billy Blizzard's fortress. The snowman groans. Jack, though, agrees with Rupert, so Rupert leads the way down in a wide sweep and lands behind the ridge of ice. The three friends dismount at once and scramble up to the top in order to spy out the land. The snowman stays put, dismally gazing after them and snivelling quietly to himself.

When they reach the top of the ridge, Rupert, Rika and Jack gaze glumly at the sight that greets them. Between the ice slabs and the fortress is a stretch of open ground, then a moat, filled with ice spears. Above the walls a blizzard rages wildly. "I just can't see a way of getting in," Jack sighs. "Nor can I," declares Rika. "We may not have to get in at all," says Rupert. All we need to do to free the snowmen is to make Billy Blizzard come out!"

"We can't sit in the snow and wait.
Our snowy friend must act as bait!"

"Good plan," says Jack. "I can see that.
But Snowman's such a scaredy-cat."

And, true to form, when he is told,
The silly Snowman's far from bold.

"Your friends depend on what you do,"
Says Rupert. "Their best hope is you!"

"How?" asks Jack. "We have to tempt him," says Rupert and points to the dismal snowman waiting below. "I'm sure Billy Blizzard won't be able to resist a chance to recapture the prisoner he lost on the way from Nutwood!" "But that cowardly snowman will never agree to act as bait!" says Rika. "We must try!" says Jack. "Our only hope is to lure Billy out, then grab him and make him hand over all the snowmen." "Come on," he calls. "Let's make a start!"

The snowman is aghast when he hears Rupert's plan. "You must be potty!" he gasps. "I only just escaped being one of his slaves!" Seeing that the others are about to lose their tempers with the timid snowman, Rupert makes a last appeal for help. "I know it's asking an awful lot," he says, "but it's the only way your fellow snowmen can be saved from a miserable life of slavery under a cruel and wicked master." The snowman gulps but says nothing.

watches the snowman

The Snowman speaks, with knocking knees.
"I have to do it," he agrees.

We'll flush The Blizzard from his lair,
Then Rika's ropes will bind him there.

So plucky Snowman squares his shoulders
And peeks around the icy boulders.

The drawbridge crashes to the ground.
And all falls silent ... not a sound ...

The snowman stares at his feet for a long time. Then he looks up at Rupert. "All right!" he says. "But I'm still scared." "Heroes often are," says Jack. "Me?" the snowman scoffs. "Not a heroic snowflake in my body." So it's agreed: the snowman will show himself on the open stretch of snow in front of the fortress. "Wait a moment," Rupert says. "What if Billy Blizzard runs inside again as soon as he sees us?" "Just let him try!" says Rika and reaches for her reindeer lasso.

Rupert and the others get into position and watch anxiously as the snowman slowly edges his way down to the open stretch of snow, keeping to the shadows as long as he can. He has been told to go just far enough into the open for Billy Blizzard to be able to see him. He pauses in the shadows at the foot of the slabs. Has he lost his nerve? No! He steps into the open and waits. For a long time nothing happens. Then, with a loud crash, the drawbridge slams down over the moat ...

RUPERT
and pals capture Billy

They all hear Billy's angry wail.
Still, Snowman's courage doesn't fail.

He stands his ground, quite brave and still,
As Rika's rope snakes down the hill.

This flying tackle's hard to beat.
It knocks our villain off his feet!

As Snowman brushes off the dust,
Billy Blizzard's tightly trussed.

Over the drawbridge charges a furious Billy Blizzard. He brandishes an icicle dart but the snowman stands his ground. Rupert and the others, who have been crouching out of sight, jump up into view. Billy casts them a wild glance but, before he can do anything, Rika swings her lasso round in the air and drops it over his shoulders. He squeals and starts to run back to the drawbridge, jerking Rika off her feet and dragging her along with him.

Rupert and Jack scramble after Rika to try and rescue her. They needn't worry though, for the snowman launches himself at Billy, bowling him over and sending his icicle dart flying. Rika picks herself up and the others join her. In no time at all Billy Blizzard has been soundly trussed up. Jack hauls him to his feet and points towards the fortress. "We're all going inside now," he snaps. "And you're coming with us, whether you like it or not!"

He snarls and fizzes furiously,
As Jack collects the dungeon key.

Then hordes of happy Snowmen pour
From Billy Blizzard's dungeon door.

"You've saved them, but you're out of luck.
There's no wind here. You're really stuck!"

But Rika laughs, "Ignore the weather.
We'll tie the Snowmen's scarves together."

Billy Blizzard snarls with rage but lets himself be led into the fortress. "Where are the snowmen?" demands Jack, taking a set of keys from the pouch on Billy's belt. Billy nods towards a nearby door. Jack unlocks it and goes through, together with the snowman. It's hard to see how Billy could look any angrier, but he scowls even more as a great cheer comes from the other room. Out march a gaggle of snowmen, with Jack and the brave snowman perched on their shoulders.

Although he's been outsmarted, Billy Blizzard isn't finished yet. As the cheering dies down he turns to Jack and sneers, "Very clever. But how will you get the snowmen to your father's palace? You can't just summon a wind like you would in the top half of the world!" "Don't worry, Jack!" cries Rika. "We'll go back to Nutwood the way we came …" The pals look puzzled, but Rika has a plan. "Collect the snowmen's scarves and knot them into three ropes," she calls.

Though Rika's clearly thought it through,
The others haven't got a clue!

Then Rupert cries. "I've been a dope!
These scarves will make a fine tow-rope"

The Snowmen know just what to do.
They form a neat and smiling queue.

"I'll leave this spike to cut you free.
But don't you dare to follow me."

Mystified by Rika's request, Rupert and Jack hurry to do as she asks while she brings the reindeer round to the flat area in front of the fort. Then, as everyone looks on, she ties a scarf 'rope' to each of the reindeer's saddles. "Now I understand!" cries Rupert. "We're going to tow the snowmen all the way back to Nutwood!" "That's right," laughs Rika. "The reindeer will do it easily. A few snowmen weigh next to nothing, compared with Santa's loaded sleigh."

At last all is ready for the journey back to Nutwood, where Jack will be able to summon a wind to carry him and the snowmen on to King Frost's palace. The snowmen are split into three groups and each given a 'rope' to hold. Before climbing onto his reindeer, Jack takes Billy Blizzard's icicle dart and sticks it upright in the snow. "You can cut yourself free as soon as we've gone," he tells him. "Don't try to follow us or you'll have my father's ice guards to deal with!"

leads the way

They soar off at a cracking pace,
Ignoring Billy's grumpy face.

"First stop Nutwood," Jack calls out.
While happy Snowmen swirl about.

Then, in the glow of morning light,
Nutwood Common comes in sight.

They find a high spot to set down,
Out of sight of Nutwood town.

"Ready?" asks Rika. Rupert and Jack nod and she gives a shrill cry. The reindeer start trotting across the flat snow, gradually gathering speed until they bound into the air, towing the snowmen behind them. "Nutwood next stop!" laughs Rupert as they race through the sky. "The snowmen and I will go straight on as soon as we arrive in Nutwood, " says Jack. "I'm afraid I'll have to go home soon too," adds Rika. "I've got to get the reindeer back to Lapland."

The light begins to grow and after a while Rupert starts to recognise the landscape down below. "Nutwood!" he cries and points excitedly to the village. "Make sure you don't land on the high common," says Jack. "We don't want anyone to see." Rika nods and down they start to go. The reindeer land so gently that all the snowmen are able to keep their feet as they slowly touch down. "We made it!" shouts Rupert happily. Everyone grins with delight, even the snowmen.

RUPERT
and Rika say goodbye

"My snowy friends and I must go,
We're very grateful, as you know."

Jack sounds his whistle, loud and high,
And off they blow, into the sky.

Says Rika, "I'll return some day.
Perhaps I'll have a peaceful stay!"

"Yes", Pong-Ping laughs. "It won't be boring.
We'd only just begun exploring!"

Jack wastes no time in gathering the snowmen around him. Then he turns to Rika and Rupert and thanks them for all their help. "Thanks from my father too!" he calls as he bids them a final farewell. I know he will be grateful for everything you've done." Taking a tiny whistle from the pouch on his belt, he gives the snowmen a sign to get ready. As soon as he blows the whistle a great wind starts to blow and whisks all the snowmen up into the air and out of sight.

That evening, as soon as it is dark, it is Rika's turn to say goodbye. She has already thanked Rupert's parents and is back in Pong-Ping's garden, ready to leave. "You really must come for a longer visit next time," Pong-Ping urges her. "I promise I shall," Rika laughs and mounts her reindeer. "Up and away!" she cries and blows a kiss to the two pals as the whole herd takes off into the night sky. "She is nice!" sigh Pong-Ping and Rupert together.

THE END

RUPERT

*It's time for a short holiday
At Pong-Ping's house, a mile away.*

Rupert is off to spend the weekend with his chum, the Peke, Pong-Ping, whose house lies on the other side of Nutwood village. The quickest way there is through the grounds of Nutwood Court. The grounds are private but the house has stood empty so long that Rupert and his pals have got used to treating them as a short cut and so, as he's done so often, Rupert climbs the stile into the overgrown grounds.

and Little Yum

*But Rupert crosses private ground
To take a short cut he has found.*

*Until a voice growls, "That will do.
I've got a bone to pick with you!"*

Rupert's mind is so much on the weekend ahead that he almost jumps out of his skin when a heavy hand falls on his shoulder and a rough voice cries, "Gotcha!" The hand belongs to a large unpleasant man. "Can't you read?" he growls, pointing back at the 'Private' sign. "Oh, please, I didn't know ... I thought ..." Rupert stammers. "Enough!" the man cries. "You're trespassing, that's what. You're coming with me!"

*"Which bit of 'Private' can't you see?
You'll have to come along with me."*

RUPERT
meets Sir Jasper

Poor Rupert's dragged between the trees,
With worried face and knocking knees.

And, with a growing sense of doom,
He's taken to Sir Jasper's room.

At once, he wants to leave this place.
Sir Jasper has a nasty face.

"You trespassed on my private land,"
Sir Jasper snarls, "And that is banned!"

"Come with you?" cries Rupert. "Why? Where?" But the man's only answer is to grab Rupert's wrist and march him towards the house. "You can't do this!" Rupert protests. "Oh, yes I can!" the man growls. "This is private property. You've no right here and now you're going to see my master. He'll decide what's to be done with you." With that he propels Rupert up the steps and into the house where he halts at a door and knocks on it.

"Come in!" snaps a voice. The man removes his cap before opening the door and pushing Rupert ahead of him. A man is standing at the fireplace, more smartly dressed than Rupert's captor but just as unpleasant looking. "Caught this one in the grounds sir," the big man says. "I meant no harm," Rupert begins. "I didn't know anyone was living here." "Quiet!" barks the slim man. "You were trespassing in my grounds and I will simply not put up with that!"

"But as this is your first offence,
Go now, and next time, have more sense."

"Your nasty little friends should know
That they're not welcome here. Now, go!"

That basement looks more like a jail
And Rupert hears a mournful wail.

Scrogg says it's just a noisy cat.
No more, no less, and that is that.

Rupert tries not to look as scared as he feels. "Oh, please," he begs. "Let me go. I'd no idea you'd moved into the house. It's been empty so long." "Quiet!" the man snaps again. He makes a show of thinking then he says, "I shall let you go just this once. But in return you shall tell all your friends they must stay off my land if they know what's good for them." Rupert nods eagerly. "Then Scrogg here will show you off the property," the man dismisses him.

Scrogg who plainly is some sort of servant of Nutwood Court's new owner marches Rupert out of the house. "You're lucky," he growls. Sir Jasper ain't usually so gentle with trespassers. So you just do what he said." Just then as they pass a small dark basement window Rupert hears a wail. "What's that?" he asks. "It came from there." He points to the basement. "Nothing to worry you," snaps Scrogg. "Cats most like." And he bundles Rupert roughly away from the spot.

But Rupert's sure that it's a lie.
It sounded like a baby's cry.

"Push off!" says Scrogg. "Don't come back here.
Don't even try to interfere."

"I'll tell Pong-Ping my curious tale
Of Scrogg and the mysterious wail."

As Rupert greets Pong-Ping at last,
Two sombre gentlemen walk past.

Even as he's being marched back to the stile where he came in Rupert can't free his mind of that wail from the basement. "It sounds like someone lost or lonely," he thinks. "Certainly wasn't a cat." As Scrogg sees him over the stile, with a warning to stay on the other side of it from now on, Rupert says what he's been thinking. Scrogg's face darkens. "Forget it. You'll find it safer to let things be," he snarls. Rupert shivers as he sets off for Pong-Ping's house.

As he hurries along, he wonders what Pong-Ping will make of all this – the man Scrogg, Sir Jasper and that doleful wail from the basement. There's something very odd going on there. "And something strange here as well," he murmurs as he turns into Pong-Ping's garden. His pal is seeing off two smartly suited men. They give Rupert a suspicious glance as they pass him.

*"These men came here to talk to me.
They seek a stranger here, you see."*

*"A stranger?" Rupert says. "How queer –
I've just met two while walking here!"*

*The mystery intrigues the boys.
Especially the funny noise.*

*But, as they head for bed that night.
They know that something isn't right.*

"I say, who are they?" whispers Rupert as the two men disappear. "I'm not quite sure," the Peke replies. "They are from the Far High Mountains of my country. They speak almost no English and so someone in Nutwood sent them to me because, apart from our pal Tigerlily and her father the Conjurer who are away at the moment, I'm the only Chinese speaker around here. They asked if any stranger has come to live here recently." "I've just met two!" Rupert says.

Now, if there's one thing Pong-Ping likes, it's a mystery. And this looks like one. A pair of strangers turn up asking about newcomers to Nutwood and now Rupert says he knows of two. So as soon as Rupert is settled with a glass of milk the Peke demands his story. "And you're sure it wasn't a cat you heard?" he asks when Rupert is done. "Certain!" he's told. Later as he is showing Rupert where he's to sleep he says, "Something's wrong here. We must tell the police tomorrow!"

RUPERT
appeals to PC Growler

But PC Growler's not impressed.
He always thinks that he knows best.

"Sir Jasper knows far more than you.
He catches creatures for the zoo."

But Growler's story doesn't fit.
Pong-Ping is not convinced one bit.

So, with some fear and trepidation,
They launch their own investigation.

Next morning Rupert and Pong-Ping hurry into Nutwood and pour out to PC Growler, the village policeman, the story of the wailing Rupert heard at Nutwood Court. "So we think you should look into it," Pong-Ping adds. "Oh, you do?" snaps Growler who dislikes being told what to do. "Well, let me tell you," he says, rising and ushering the two outside, "Sir Jasper is a highly respected trapper of animals for zoos. So be off with you. And stay off private property!"

"Oh, dear, we must have made a mistake," Rupert says as he and Pong-Ping walk away from the police station. "Mistake nothing!" snorts the Peke. "Just because that man at Nutwood Court is a sir and 'highly respected' Growler thinks there can't be anything wrong. Well, we think there is, so if Growler won't investigate we shall. We'll go there after dark tonight." Just then they pass Nutwood Court looming over the trees. "Oh, do you really think we should?" Rupert quavers.

RUPERT
and Pong-Ping explore

Pong-Ping is full of plans and schemes.
He's sure that all's not as it seems.

Though Rupert Bear has knocking knees,
They must do something, he agrees.

As night falls, quiet as a mouse,
They creep up to Sir Jasper's house.

They hear a cry that's sad and low.
And light flows from the steps below.

Rupert keeps fretting about Pong-Ping's plan to investigate Nutwood Court that night. He's far from happy about it and as they reach the Peke's house he says so: "After all, Sir Jasper and PC Growler have warned us about trespassing. I think we should leave well alone." "But, Rupert," snaps Pong-Ping as they arrive back at his house. "We both think something's wrong there. If you won't come I'll go alone." "Oh," sighs Rupert. "I suppose ..."

And so that night our pair set out for Nutwood Court. Even the Peke whose idea this is, isn't so keen now that the time has come. But with Pong-Ping carrying a lantern and Rupert leading the way, they steal into the grounds of the old house. The night is light enough for them to do without the lantern as they make their way into the basement where Rupert heard the wailing. They are almost there when they stop in their tracks. There is a glow of light from the basement steps.

RUPERT

hears the noise again

Where Scrogg is banging on the door.
And shouting "Stop it! Cry no more!"

And, as they ponder what he said,
Scrogg storms inside to go to bed.

The night is dark, the night is cold
Poor Pong-Ping does not feel so bold.

But Rupert's courage does not fail.
He runs towards the mournful wail.

The pals creep forward to the shelter of a bush and from there they can see the glow is from a lamp held by the servant Scrogg. Then they freeze as a heart-broken wail rises from inside the basement. "Quiet!" Scrogg snarls. "And stay quiet if you know what's good for you." With that he whacks the door with his stick, stomps up the basement steps and goes back to the house. The front door slams and then there is silence. Rupert and Pong-Ping exchange looks.

Rupert can see that the wailing from the basement and the sight of the unpleasant Scrogg have had their effect on Pong-Ping who now looks a great deal less brave. "D-do you think we should go back?" he quavers. Rupert is just as scared but he shakes his head. "We can't," he hisses. "Not after that wail." Pong-Ping gulps and murmurs, "You're right." Just then the last light in the house goes out. "Now," Rupert says and they dash for the basement steps.

RUPERT
find a baby Yeti

He listens at the basement door.
And wonders what could be in store.

They hear a small and frightened squeak.
The door swings, with a ghostly creak.

The chums can only gasp and look.
It's something from a story-book

The baby Yeti's terrified
As Pong-Ping brings the light inside.

Rupert and Pong-Ping reach the basement steps safely. They hold their breath. Will there be a sudden angry shout, a blaze of light from the house? No, Nutwood Court stays silent and dark. So they tiptoe down the steps. The door into the basement is a heavy affair with a bolt on the outside – luckily without a padlock. They listen. "Who's in there?" Rupert whispers as loudly as he dare. The answer is a gulp. The Peke switches on the lantern. They open the door ...

Rupert and Pong-Ping stand speechless. The beam of their lantern reveals, cowering against the far wall, a creature such as Rupert has never imagined, still less seen. It's smaller than he is and covered in fur from the top of its pointy head to the toes peeping from the bottom of its little legs. Its eyes are big and startled as it tries to make out the figure from behind the light. "I can't believe this," Pong-Ping breathes. "It's a-a baby Yeti!"

95

RUPERT

plans an escape

Pong-Ping has Yeti-lore to tell.
"They're tall and strong, but shy as well."

"This little Yeti's very cute
And worth a lot of cash, to boot."

Although he's frightened, cold and pale
They lead him from the basement jail.

But, as they tiptoe safely out,
A sneeze escapes the Yeti's snout.

"A Yeti?" repeats Rupert. The Peke nods. "Yeti live in the highest mountains of my country," he says. "So few outsiders have seen one that many don't believe they exist. They grow big and look fearsome. In fact, they're very shy and are highly honoured by our mountain folk who'd do anything to protect them." He sighs: "But to some awful people a baby one like this would be worth a fortune." The little creature sobs.

Pong-Ping pats its head and says "There, there." The baby Yeti sniffs hard and stops sobbing. "We must get it out of here," urges Rupert. "Right," says Pong-Ping and takes the Yeti's hand and whispers something in Chinese. "I said it will be safe with us and must be very quiet," he explains. "But I don't think it understands." Still, the Yeti is as quiet as the others as they start up the steps. Quiet, that is, until the Yeti sneezes! "Oh, no!" gasp Rupert and Pong-Ping.

RUPERT

flees from Nutwood Court

That sneeze means trouble – there's no doubt.
A torchlight beam soon picks them out.

They hear Sir Jasper's rasping tones.
"Get up, Scrogg! Shift your idle bones!"

The chase is on. They must escape.
Or Yum will be back in a scrape.

But Scrogg and Jasper run, they know,
Far faster than Yum's legs will go.

For a moment after the little Yeti's sneezing there is an awful silence. Rupert and the others hold their breath. Did anyone in the house hear it? They are beginning to think they may have been lucky when a window shoots up and they find themselves pinned in the beam of a powerful torch. Then Sir Jasper's voice rings out: "I see them! After them Scrogg!" Rupert and Pong-Ping exchange horrified looks. The baby Yeti looks pleadingly up at them.

Lights come on in Nutwood Court and there is a clatter of feet as the two men race for the front door. "Quick!" cries Rupert. "To the stile!" At Rupert's cry Pong-Ping springs into life and, clasping the little Yeti's hands, they make a run for it. The Yeti's little legs cannot keep up, but he is safely hustled along by the pals. But, fast as they are moving, they hear their pursuers getting closer. "Over here!" hisses Rupert and drags the others into the bushes.

RUPERT

hides in a bush

They dive behind a bush to hide
And crouch in silence, side by side.

It works! The villains blunder past.
The chums think that they're safe at last.

The garden gate's not far away.
They'll live to fight another day!

Alas, they find out, with a groan.
That, once again, they're not alone.

"Where are you taking us?" pants Pong-Ping. But Rupert only hisses, "Shh! Get down both of you!" and pulls the pair of them down behind a clump of bushes. "And keep quiet!" At that moment the baby Yeti takes a deep breath as if it might sneeze again. Pong-Ping clamps a hand over its mouth and makes urgent Chinese sounds. It nods as if it understands and the Peke takes his hand away. A moment later Sir Jasper and Scrogg dash past, heading for the stile.

Rupert waits until the men are well past then whispers to Pong-Ping, "Now we've got to reach the old gate before they find they've been fooled." The old gate is the main entrance to the grounds and is where Rupert was headed when Scrogg stopped him. Pong-Ping makes comforting sounds to the baby Yeti then he and Rupert take its hand and the three make a dash for the gate. They reach it, squeeze through – and cry out at the sight that greets them.

RUPERT

listens to Pong-Ping's tale

For, looking rather stern again,
Are Pong-Ping's frowning gentlemen.

They grab both Peke and Rupert Bear
And whisk them up into the air.

Yum squeaks and chatters, to explain.
The men put Rupert down again.

Our chums are friends, they realise.
And, promptly, they apologise.

Looming in the light of Pong-Ping's lamp are the two men who came to his house asking about the newcomers to Nutwood. "They must have heard about Sir Jasper being new," thinks Rupert. "That will be why they are here." The strangers stare bleakly at the pals. One of them hisses angrily at Pong-Ping in Chinese. But before the Peke can reply he is grabbed by the man and swung off his feet. The other man lunges for Rupert and gathers him up struggling.

Suddenly the baby Yeti lets loose a torrent of high-pitched chatter. At once the pals are put down – respectfully. The men bow and one addresses Pong-Ping. The Peke translates: "They have come from the Far High Mountains to rescue the baby Yeti – his name is Yum and he was stolen from there. They traced him to Nutwood and when they saw us with him they thought we were the ones who took him. But now Yum has told them what really happened."

RUPERT

has a plan

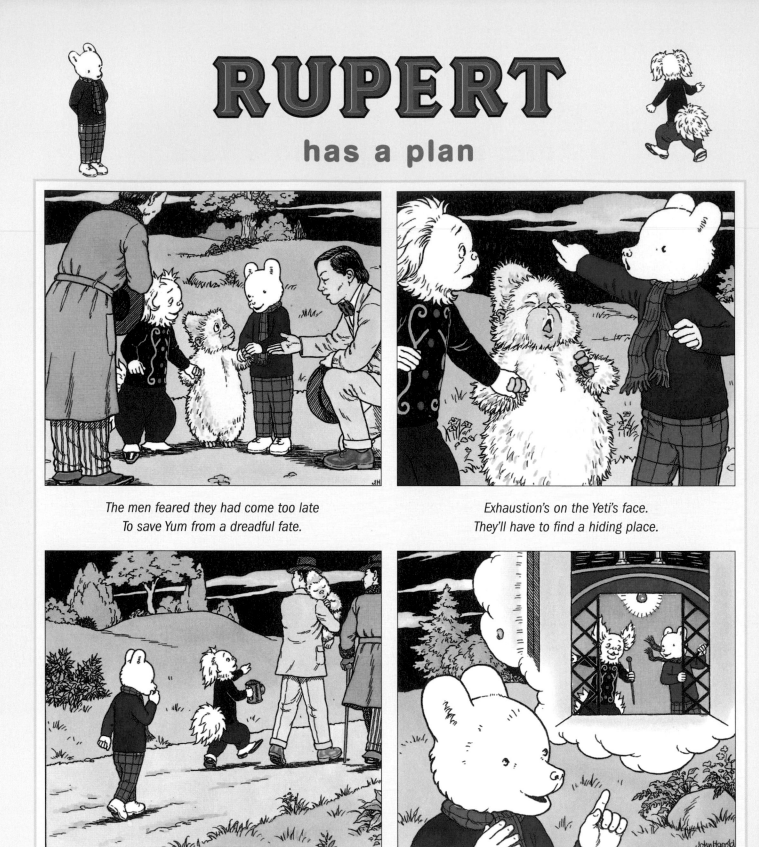

*The men feared they had come too late
To save Yum from a dreadful fate.*

*Exhaustion's on the Yeti's face.
They'll have to find a hiding place.*

*Yum slumbers on the gentleman,
While Rupert makes a rescue plan.*

*Pong-Ping's lift goes straight through the earth,
To China, and Yum's place of birth.*

Rupert looks on bewildered as Yum and one of the men chatter quickly in Yeti talk. He then translates into Chinese for Pong-Ping who tells Rupert: "The men want to find Sir Jasper and punish him and Yum wants to know what we think." "It's more important to get Yum away from here at once," says Rupert. "The best place is your house." "You're right," the Peke agrees. And just then Yum begins to yawn and yawn.

When Yum has been told what the pals think and has agreed, the little party sets out for Pong-Ping's house with one of the men carrying little Yum who is now fast asleep. As they go Rupert wonders how the three can be got safely away from Nutwood and Sir Jasper. Then – got it! Pong-Ping's lift! In case you don't know Nutwood well, it should be explained that the Peke has a lift in his garden that goes right through the world, all the way to the part of China he comes from.

leaves Yum to sleep

Pong-Ping agrees the plan is sound
And Yum will soon be homeward bound.

But Yum's new chums will not proceed
Until the Yeti has agreed.

They tuck Yum in and let him sleep.
The Yeti doesn't make a peep!

A sleepy Rupert climbs the stairs.
"I'll check the lift," Pong-Ping declares.

"Just what I was thinking!" cries Pong-Ping when Rupert mentions his idea of using the lift to get Yum and the others safely away. But there's to be no putting the plan to work this night. For though the men think the plan splendid – despite finding it hard to believe in the lift – they say firmly that Yum must be asked if he agrees. "Then wake him and ask," urges the Peke. "Impossible!" he's told. Baby Yeti, it seems, must be left to waken when they are ready.

There's nothing for it, then, but to wait for Yum to waken in his own time. The men say they are sorry, but it's just out of the question to take a so-honoured Yeti on any journey to China without its approval. So with Yum tucked up on a couch and the two men keeping watch, the pals decide to get some sleep too. "Go on up," Pong-Ping tells Rupert. "I'll make sure the lift's working before I go to bed."

RUPERT

is in trouble

"Wake up, you sleepy Rupert! Shift!
Yum's ready for the Chinese lift!"

They hear a knock – and turn to stare.
Then Rupert goes to see who's there.

Scrogg looms beside his nasty boss.
With PC Growler, who looks cross.

Poor Little Yum is filled with fear.
"Aw," Growler says. "Poor little dear."

It is morning when Rupert is wakened by Pong-Ping. The Peke has been up some time and is full of his news. "Little Yum has agreed to go home by my lift," he announces happily. "The men asked him as soon as he woke and he said, yes." "Then let's get moving now!" Rupert says. I'll get dressed and join you downstairs." When he goes down the others are waiting for him. As he arrives there is a knock on the front door. Being nearest, Rupert opens it ...

"They're the ones who took my valuable wild beast, constable!" Sir Jasper's angry words and accusing finger greet Rupert. PC Growler looks stern between Sir Jasper and Scrogg who is carrying a net. "Make him hand it over!" Sir Jasper cries. "Yum isn't a wild beast!" protests Rupert. "He's just a baby ..." "Best to take a look at this," rumbles PC Growler stepping inside. Sir Jasper and Scrogg plainly weren't expecting this. They exchange troubled looks.

102

RUPERT

explains all to Growler

Poor Little Yum is filled with fear.
"Aw," Growler says. "Poor little dear."

The chums let PC Growler know
That they did let the Yeti go.

To set the sorry creature free
And send him to his family.

Pong-Ping is both surprised and miffed,
When Growler asks to see the lift.

When he sees Sir Jasper and Scrogg follow PC Growler indoors Yum squeaks and hops behind one of the men. "Ahh! Poor little thing ..." Growler starts. He corrects himself: "Harrumph! Now, Rupert, did you take this gent's wild ... (He pauses and looks at little Yum) ... animal?" "He's not wild!" Rupert repeats hotly. "He's a baby Yeti who ought never to have been captured. And, yes, I took him because he was so miserable." "So did I!" Pong-Ping cries.

"You see! Those two did take my Yeti!" snarls Sir Jasper. "Only to take him back to his home in the Far High Chinese Mountains!" Pong-Ping retorts. "Oh, and how were you going to get there?" PC Growler asks. "Why, by my private lift," Pong-Ping says. "A lift to China!" exclaims Growler. "Never heard of such a thing. Let's have a look at it!" He motions the Peke to lead the way. "That's very odd," thinks Rupert. "I know that Growler knows about Pong-Ping's lift."

RUPERT

is confused by Growler

They can't imagine what's in store,
For Growler's seen the lift before!

They squeeze into the tiny room,
While Scrogg and Jasper stand and fume.

"Oh dear, that isn't what I meant.
I bumped that knob by accident!"

The villains look on in dismay,
The lift is clearly on its way.

Pong-Ping leads the way to the lift, wondering like Rupert, why Growler is acting as if he has never heard of the lift before. He enters the lift with Growler who makes a great show of gazing around. As he does so he rests his hand on a lever. "Hey, careful," cries Pong-Ping. "That starts it!" The PC lifts his hand. "Surely you couldn't all get into this?" he questions. "It's bigger than it looks," Pong-Ping replies. "Let's see," Growler says. The Peke beckons to the two men and Yum inside.

Nervously they step inside the lift. It's a bit of a squeeze, but once they're settled there's still some space. "I am astonished," Growler admits. "Why, we could fit you in as well, Rupert," he marvels. "Let's try." Puzzled, Rupert squeezes in as Sir Jasper and Scrogg look on, wondering what Growler's up to. "Careful!" Growler gasps, "Or you'll be pushing me against the starter lever ... oh, oh, you have!" There is a deep humming and the lift starts to move!

RUPERT
and pals whizz to China

It seems that Growler's small 'mistake'
Was made to give the chums a break!

And, as the lift turns upside-down
They see that Growler's no one's clown.

The little Yeti squeaks with glee,
For home is where he wants to be.

But still, there is one final test.
Does Growler still plan to arrest?

"Oh, dear!" cries Growler as the lift speeds towards China. Yet he neither looks nor sounds as upset as one might expect. "What have I done?" he adds. "I know what you have done," thinks Rupert. "You have been a rather crafty and very kindly policeman." And he's sure Pong-Ping has the same idea. But now the Peke speaks in Chinese to the two men. "I've told them the lift turns over about now so that we reach China the right way up," he explains. "Ready – now!"

At last the lift stops. "China!" Pong-Ping announces. Rupert and the others step out into daylight. "China!" PC Growler repeats. "Well, I never!" Just then Yum spies the distant mountains and squeaks with glee. Somewhere among them is his home. Then he stops, looks solemn and squawks inquiringly. There is a burst of Chinese between the two men and Pong-Ping who turns to Growler. "They want to know if you are going to arrest them?" he explains. Growler sighs.

RUPERT
says goobye to Yum

But Growler grins, "You need not fear.
For I'm not a policeman here!"

"You're free to go." He tells the men.
"Safe travels 'til we meet again."

They head towards the shining sun.
A sight that pleases everyone,

Except for Jasper and for Scrogg.
Yes, Growler is a wily dog!

"Oh, I can't arrest anyone here," Growler says in a regretful tone. "I'd have to get a local policeman to do that and by the time I found one Yum and the others would be miles away." Rupert grins at Pong-Ping. "Tell them that," he says. "Especially the bit about being 'miles away'." Pong-Ping laughs and addresses the two men. They smile broadly and bow to Growler and the pals before taking little Yum's hands and turning towards the mountains.

"Escaping, as I feared they would," sighs Growler, as Yum and the two men disappear into the distance. "We can tell everyone you did all you could," says Rupert with a straight face. "And you did follow the case all the way to China," adds the Peke. "So I did," agrees Growler. "Not bad for a village policeman really. Now I think we'd best all go home." So the three get back into Pong-Ping's lift. As they do, Growler winks at the others.

THE END

1st Prize

'Captain Rupert' kindly donated by Royal Doulton

Captain Rupert is supplied by Royal Doulton. It makes up part of a limited edition of only 2,500 copies. For more information on Rupert products by Royal Doulton, please visit: www.royaldoulton.com

2nd Prize

Rupert 1958 Facsimile
Collector's Annual kindly donated by the
Official Rupert Bear Shop

This collector's limited edition 1958 Rupert Annual, presented in a protective hard slipcase and with a certificate of authentication will be a treasured possession for years to come. For more information on Rupert merchandise, please visit: www.officialrupertbearshop.com

3rd Prize

Rupert Bear scarf

This beautiful Merino and Cashmere Wool is an official Rupert Bear scarf that is one-size.

Prizewinners will be notified by post by 31 March 2007 and prizes will be forwarded after this date.

This competition is open to readers of up to and including 10 years of age on 31 January 2007. The competition closing date is 31 January 2007 so all entries must be received by then to be considered. Do make sure the form and the picture do not get detached. Please read the rules on the reverse of this page very carefully to make sure your entry will be accepted.

Enjoy colouring this Rupert picture, then enter the competition. *Fill in your details on the back of this page.*

Colouring Competition

Colouring Competition

RULES FOR ENTRY

1. Age and neatness will be taken into consideration in the judging process.
2. You may use pens, pencils, paints or crayons to colour your entry.
3. No entries will be accepted after the closing date.
4. No entries will be accepted without a parent's or guardian's signature to prove the colouring is all your own work.
5. The competition is open to all UK residents aged 10 or under (as of 31 January 2007) other than employees of and relations of employees of Northern & Shell Media, Express Newspapers, Entertainment Rights, the printers and distributors, Royal Doulton and other associated companies.
6. Only one entry per person.
7. There are no cash alternatives to the prizes above.
8. The judges' decision is final; unfortunately no entries can be returned.
9. Express Newspapers reserve the right to use the winning entries for publicity.
10. Express Newspapers cannot accept responsibility for lost, delayed or damaged entries.
11. All entries to be sent to:

    Rupert Bear Colouring Competition 2006,
    Express Newspapers,
    Northern & Shell Building,
    Number 10 Lower Thames Street,
    London EC3R 6EN

ENTRY FORM

Please do not detatch this form from the picture
Please fill in form in block capitals:

NAME

ADDRESS

POSTCODE

TELEPHONE NUMBER

E-MAIL ADDRESS

AGE AS OF 31 JAN 2007

I certify that this entry is work by entrant only

Signature of Parent or Guardian

Please make sure you have read all the rules and are in agreement.

Follow Rupert

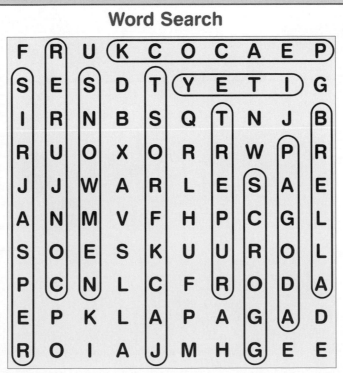

in the DAILY✚EXPRESS
and the SUNDAY✚EXPRESS

John Harrold.

Answers to Puzzles

Word Search

F	R	U	K	C	O	C	A	E	P
S	E	S	D	T	Y	E	T	I	G
I	R	N	B	S	Q	T	N	J	B
R	U	O	X	O	R	R	W	P	R
J	J	W	A	R	L	E	S	A	E
A	N	M	V	F	H	P	C	G	L
S	O	E	S	K	U	U	R	O	L
P	C	N	L	C	F	R	O	D	A
E	P	K	L	A	P	A	G	A	D
R	O	I	A	J	M	H	G	E	E

The publisher would like to thank the following for their assistance in compiling this book: John Harrold; Gina Hart; Entertainment Rights Plc, Alan Murray; Gary Barrell; Royal Doulton; Michael Trew; The British Origami Society; Phil Toze; Sheila Reed. All rights reserved. No part of this publication may be reproduced, stored in a retrieval system, or transmitted in any form or by any means, electronic, mechanical, photocopying, recording or otherwise, without written permission from the copyright owner, Entertainment Rights Distribution Limited/Express Newspapers.
Colour reproduction by Wyndeham-Icon. Printed by Rotolito, Italy.

John Harrold.